THE GRAND SISTER
OF THE NIGHT

THE GRAND
VIZIER OF
THE NIGHT

CATHERINE HERMARY-VIEILLE

Translated by

CHARLES PENWARDEN

QUARTET BOOKS

First published in English in 1988 by
Quartet Books Limited
A member of the Namara Group
27 Goodge Street, London WIT 2LD
This paperback edition published in 2014

First published in France as *Le Grand Vizir de la Nuit*

A catalogue record for this book
is available from the British Library

ISBN   978 0 7043 7345 7

Typeset Antony Gray
Printed and bound in Great Britain by
TJ International, Padstow, Cornwall

CONTENTS

The Arab-Islamic World at the end of the tenth century

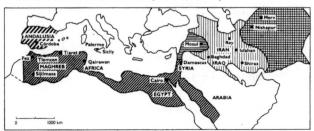

- ▨ Omayyads of Spain
- ▩ Fatimid Caliphate
- ▤ Hamdanids ⎤
- ▥ Buyids   ⎬ Abbasid Caliphate
- ▦ Samanids ⎦

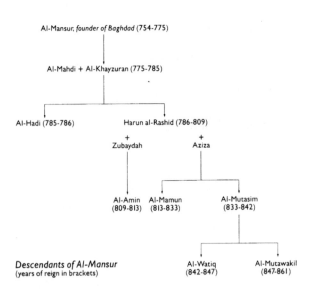

Al-Mansur, *founder of Baghdad* (754-775)

Al-Mahdi + Al-Khayzuran (775-785)

Al-Hadi (785-786)

Harun al-Rashid (786-809)
+
Zubaydah
+
Aziza

Al-Amin
(809-813)

Al-Mamun
(813-833)

Al-Mutasim
(833-842)

Descendants of Al-Mansur
(years of reign in brackets)

Al-Watiq
(842-847)

Al-Mutawakil
(847-861)

GLOSSARY

abaya	gown
aggal	rope which secures the head-dress
babouche	oriental slipper made of leather or fabric
burdah	woollen coat or gown, a more prestigious version of the *abaya*
chador	veil
cithara	musical instrument which resembles the lyre
faience golestan	mythical Persian bird pictured in porcelain
galabiya	long, loose garment with a hood
jebel	hill or mountain
kuffiya	cloth worn on the head as part of the head-dress
madrasa	a Quranic school
maqsurah	small palace or luxurious royal apartment
mashrabiyah	carved wooden screen over windows in oriental buildings to protect the privacy of women's chambers
mehara	thoroughbred dromedary
meharis	a company of the above, mounted by the Caliph's guard
muezzin	the crier who calls the faithful to prayer five times a day
Ramadan	Muslim holy month
suq	Arab market
vermeil	gilded metal, usually silver

If the minister grows to equal the king in wealth, prestige and authority, then the king must throw him out of office; if not, he must know that he himself will be overthrown.

IBN QUTAYBA

PROLOGUE

A long long time ago, years and centuries, in the round town with three walls, the town of salvation, in the middle of this gift of God on earth, in the red and ochre dust of a summer's afternoon, an old beggar, a poor and humble man, was waiting for death. He was so old, so wrinkled, so like the walls of yellow brick that girt the town with three proud ramparts, that he melted into them like a gold coin at sunset. Ahmed was waiting for death. With him would die the memories of an ancient time.

Many years ago now, on the bridge where they had spiked it, the head of Ja'far al-Barmaki had crumbled to dust. Time, the heat, and the birds had overcome that beauty and that pride. Ahmed thought back to past times. Often had he passed the mortal remains of that man he had so passionately loved. Often had he proffered silent greetings, silent in fear of the spies who were all about the town, silent before the eyes and ears of the absent caliph, Al Mutawakil. Ja'far was dead, dead the light of those eyes, dead those lips, parched that warm saliva; that brown skin, so soft to the finger's touch, was dead; those delicately stroking hands were dead; that burning voice, husky and caressing like an eastern wind, was dead. How could he remember? How could he vomit up this aftermath, this poison which had not even killed him, but merely expelled him from the mouth of the past, leaving him in rags in the streets of Baghdad, counting the days and the years that still kept him from his master.

So many days, so many years, so many summers of hunger and thirst, so many outstretched hands and

9

beseeching voices: 'In the name of God, the Merciful One'; and so many silences.

Then, feeling death come upon him, Ahmed was fired with a passionate desire to speak. The great square of the craftsmen's quarter was growing busy at this end of a summer afternoon. Ahmed rose up straight on his folded legs; once more, he found his voice and dignity of times past, times when his bearing was upright and his speech resonant as he cut through the despised crowd, that same crowd which now scarcely stepped aside to avoid him, trampling underfoot his poverty and prostration. They were nothing to him, yet he would speak to them. He would give his final monologue to the silence of these shadows who peopled the solitude. Shadows to lower the curtain of death. No more secrets before these people, nothing but murmurs and music in the evening wind, the timbre of a voice returning to Ja'far, blowing gently through the loved one's remains on the bridge, making them shiver in the warmth of the night. Few days of life remained to him. In those few hours he would weave for his master's shroud a cloth of sweetness and tenderness to wrap him in silence, violence and hate, cries of pleasure and murmurs of love, ambitions without measure like the beauty of Ja'far. Harun al-Rashid had loved him, Harun al-Rashid had killed him. He too was dead now. All of them came together in a silent dance that flickered in the summer breeze – mobile as a shadow, elusive, vanishing.

One or two people had stopped in front of Ahmed as he began his stories of times past, of days when Baghdad, the golden city, courted its rulers the Barmakids like an amorous sultan's wife, languorous and caressing, submissive and skilled in giving pleasure; Baghdad, abandoned by its caliph, now an old and idle mistress, thick, heavy and somnolent – sterile. More and more passers-by stopped, curious to hear this storyteller from out of their past. They formed a clamorous circle, closed in upon itself like Ahmed's existence, like a crown of triumph or of death; this crowd which would take him in and rock him from word to word, words to be repeated from one generation to another, through all time.

'I lived,' said Ahmed 'in the time of your masters the Barmakids . . . '

AHMED'S FIRST NIGHT

Harun, our caliph, and Fadl, my master's brother, were suckled with the same milk; they grew up together in the palace of Al-Mahdi. The greatness of the Barmakids was renowned even then. Cast back your thoughts to that family, and let their dignity rise up from the narrow corners of your memory, breathe it out like perfume from the neck of a flask. Think back to the sultans, the Al-Barmaki. Even then, Yahya was the master. Omniscient, he could see into all things. He was a man old in wisdom before the whitening of his hairs. He looked tenderly upon the young prince and upon his own son. In his dreams, he saw them as a falcon with two heads, and with his hands he built them a kingdom. The only heritage he desired to leave them was his passion for intelligence and freedom; nobility, fortune and glory had already been laid before their feet.

Ahmed looked about him. No one was moving. In the eyes of those listening he saw a glimmer of the curiosity that appears in the eyes of children when you tell them a story, a tale of demons to which they listen in terror before sleeping. These people, perhaps they were already asleep: had they not always slept? Could even a single one of them imagine what they were like, the caliph and the princes' days in Baghdad? What could they know of the mouth and eyes of Ja'far, so languorous in pleasure, what of the mouth and eyes of Ja'far pecked hollow by birds on the bridge of Baghdad? It was the same man for the same truth – a matter of the moment and the play of

13

light; of love too, perhaps – God surely knows. In summer the dawn is sweet and sweet is the night: the infernal heat of day pours out then is quenched in a throbbing like that of a bird's heart beating as it takes to the wing.

I grew up with Ja'far al-Barmaki; we lived apart from Harun and Fadl, our elders; we lived entwined in a friendship that resembled love. Much more than the son of his serving maid, I was his friend. Together we read poems and fought bare-handed, together galloped through the red earth around Baghdad and shared the cool water at the fountainside. As youths, we looked and found ourselves beautiful, with our satiny skin, our soft sweet mouths and our light caressing hands. Who could fail to see? When he laced his body about mine, Ja'far would dream of a woman, and I would dream of Ja'far. In those summer nights we could not sleep. Remember, all of you, when you were fifteen.

One day, a nurse told us that the Berber queen, Al-Khayzuran, had called Yahya al-Barmaki to her palace. They had talked for many hours. The Berber wanted power for Harun, her younger son; the older and un-desirable Al-Hadi, the weak and cruel Al-Hadi who was deaf to his mother's wishes, had to be cast aside. The caliph must be persuaded to choose Harun as successor. Yahya loved Harun like a son; he carried him proudly like a falcon on his wrist, dreaming of the day when he would see him take flight. He would help him. Thus Yahya joined with the Berber; together they would make Harun caliph, the absolute master – their masterpiece, the golden statue chiselled out by their ambitions. Al-Mahdi was old; he no longer saw what was needed, could no longer tell the just from the unjust, what was frank from what was sly and menacing. He had loved war and violence: now he wished to rest. Al-Hadi was far away, governor of the province of Djurdjan, deaf to the rumours of Baghdad. He must be persuaded of Harun's supremacy. They would slip sweet somniferous herbs in his ears, telling him that peace between two brothers was all that mattered. Al-Khayzuran wanted it thus, and what the queen willed the caliph wanted also. He set off to see his son. With Ja'far, I watched the beginning of our master's journey, the splendid cortege in the dust of a high summer's morning. A yellow and pink dust licked about the red walls of Baghdad, about its grey minarets, and about the golden horseman astride the green dome of the royal palace. The crowd was there, gazing at the black and white horses with their gold and silver saddles, at the proud bearing of their riders – princes and officers, dignitaries and holy men. A warm wind blew from the west, wrapping the black flag of the Abbasids around its pole, while from the market wafted odours of spices and leather, of perfumes and mud. Al-Mahdi was leaving Baghdad never to see her again, leaving the garden of delights for the garden of death, like a golden ball slipping from his hands and rolling away from him for ever. For the last time, Al-Mahdi turned and looked upon his town.

Already, the shifting and turbid transparency of the midsummer heat could be seen rising on the horizon as, one by one, the horsemen disappeared into it. Only the horde of servants in their grey, black and white costumes remained visible, as if hovering between reality and imagination. Soon, they too disappeared into the dust. Viewed from the ramparts of Baghdad, it was like a dream dissolving at daybreak. We turned back to the town. During the nights of that uncertain month of July, Ja'far would gaze at the stars: 'Ahmed,' he told me, 'all is written, my father's glory or his death; all our deaths. It is all there, and yet we are unable to read it. Ignorant or blind, what difference does it make! Our gaze is turned inward.'

Fadl and Harun went for long walks in the palace gardens; sometimes they would be joined by Yahya. They had stopped laughing now; instead, they talked and reflected, they exchanged glances and knew that their destinies were all bound together – with bonds so tight, indeed, that I sometimes had the fleeting impression they were choking.

When August came, we kept to the cool of the patio and the nocturnal shivering of the wind on the terraces. We were all waiting, but for what? For our destiny perhaps. The air smelt of dust, cumin and soot, mingling from time to time with the fragrance of the Baghdad roses which, like us, had come from Persia to bloom under the skies of Iraq. Yes, you who hear me, know that the Barmakids and their servants came from Persia; that is why you did not love us. Our only fault was to be older, supreme in a wisdom which we gave you to share. We loved your country.

Ahmed stopped. He was thirsty for water and for the unspoken words he had carried within him for so long now. A man handed him a brown goatskin and he drank and gazed at the stars, the same stars as in August 168 [785AD], the very same. Nothing had changed except for the death of his masters and his own old age. So little . . . Alone now, he looked back on those times with love. Love and memory: such poor, light, perishable emotions, yet Ahmed felt he could no longer hold them back; he must release them so that he might in turn fade and dissolve into them. The night was black, and the odour of burnt wood mingled with the smell of the fritters cooking in mutton fat around the square. In an hour or two, each man would go home, would lie on his terrace with his face up to the heavens as the nightbirds warbled from atop the minarets. At dawn, life would begin again with the call to prayer.

Ahmed went on; so few days and so much still to say, so many memories and so much oblivion to extract from himself before bringing forth his own death. To make a clear space and be nothing . . . All of a sudden, a sharp, vivid image made him shudder: how could so many years evaporate in so short an instant? In a twinkling, he was at Ja'far's side, listening to some music. It was early in the morning, and a few birds were bathing in the basin in the centre of the patio. Around them the drops of water shimmered in the intense light of the summer day. Sitting against the wall, some blind musicians were drawing soft sweet music from their instruments with their fine caressing fingers. Ja'far was holding his hand and the air tasted of sandalwood and musk. Ahmed remembered it perfectly: it was a Monday, and they were eighteen years old! Then, suddenly, the sound of footsteps on the marble made them jump and withdraw their hands. Before them stood Fadl, stiff and severe. 'The caliph is dead, assassinated,' he said, and was gone. The birds had all flown away and the musicians had stopped playing. Ahmed could still hear that silence, even now: never again in his lifetime would silence be so intense. Ja'far had once again taken his hand but, instead of caressing it, he was now squeezing it violently. In the sky, the sun was rising: its light was warm and golden like honey flowing over the blue ceramic of the basin; a musician ran his fingers over his lute. 'We are lost,' said Ja'far, 'Al-Hadi will forgive us nothing.' In the middle of the basin, water gushed forth from the jade dolphin, to die in a thousand bubbles against the turquoise sides; some of them were carried over the edge and formed transparent puddles on the pink and white marble. Ja'far stood up, took some water in the hollow of his right hand and drank. His lips and eyes were shining.

'I drink to celebrate our new caliph,' he said, 'his power shall no more intoxicate me than does this beverage.'

'The musicians are listening, master,' I murmured.

'Then let them play,' he replied, 'and let the caliph reign!'

Ahmed would say nothing of this memory to his audience. He merely gave them all a look. Tired, he wanted to sleep. His life had been a dream followed by the long slumber before death. Since Ja'far was assassinated, he had never been certain that he was alive: occasionally he had the impression of life, as when he smelt the first fragrance of jasmine in spring or saw the silhouette of a falcon, black against the blue sky. At such times, he would close his eyes and block his nostrils so as to refuse this proof of a life he no longer desired. Scabies, rags and fever were the only parts of himself he still accepted. Each further stage of decay was like a gold coin to pay for Ja'far's death, a perfume to embalm his mutilated corpse, a gift of love. Once again, Ahmed tried to raise himself up, putting his hands on the ground to support his body: he opened his eyes and continued.

Al-Hadi returned to Baghdad in the dust of his galloping horses. He went to the caliph's palace and imposed his authority on those who had spurned him. The Berber queen, his mother, was sent back to her own palace, Harun and Yahya were put in prison, and Fadl and Ja'far were exiled from Baghdad. Everywhere there were murmurs and revolts – killings in the palace, the Shiites massacred – everywhere intolerance and hatred, everywhere could be seen the glittering of Al-Hadi's two gold bracelets. As for ourselves, we were waiting, we knew full well that this violence was like a sand storm that would bury the caliph. In our ochre palace, in the middle of a desert plain to the east of Baghdad, far to the east, we watched the clouds drift by and saw in them the symbol of the transience of all things. Fadl studied and read and met with men of gravity; they did not even see us, Ja'far and me – brown, slim and vigorous as we rode our horses through the red dust. We spoke with shepherds and thought that they, perhaps, were wiser than Fadl's guests. They showed us the stars and gave us sour milk and sweet tea to drink. Sometimes, on our way back to the palace, our sticky lips would come together. I dreamt that I had become him, disappeared in him. But he was already far away in thoughts of another destiny than my strong arms or warm skin, in thoughts of power and perhaps, already, of Harun. The winter was hard, we wore fur caps and looked like Mongols, but with my master, the days were long and the nights short. Fadl, his eyes full of princely contempt, pushed me aside like an animal whenever our paths crossed. He shared his bed with a woman, his wife – of noble Arab stock – and with his concubines, those attentive slaves who were always on the lookout for a chance to dominate him. I despised them all. What I desired was to serve my master, to be dedicated to his pleasure only – docile and attentive, a gift, a moment of love. Sometimes, Ja'far would look at the servant women, would laugh with them and grow serious when he had left them. I hated him then but knew that, one day, one of them would take him from me, for an instant or more, not for ever. The taste of women was heady and compelling like a drug. I felt pure. Ja'far never spoke to me of his hopes. I knew there was no place for me there.

Springtime, the first odours of jasmine: if we closed our eyes we could almost believe we were still in Baghdad. Less dust, fewer odours, another quality to the passing time. One night, Ja'far did not come to me. He was with that Afghan woman with eyes like a submissive bitch. I crushed the jasmine I had picked in my hands and rubbed it on my face to wipe away the smell of that woman. Ja'far and her, body against body, their sweat mingling and mouths joined, their sexes united. This was a kind of death for me. I did not cry: my master did as he pleased. The next day, he was with me.

Ahmed raised his eyes. Around him now, only a few children and a man, who was staring at him – a Persian; Ahmed knew, he could tell . . .

'May salvation be yours,' said the man.

'And may you too be saved,' replied the old man.

The man came up to him and held out a silver coin. When he was close to Ahmed, he murmured: 'My father was from the house of the Barmakids. Spend the night in comfort.'

'Tomorrow,' said Ahmed, 'at the same time, you may hear the following episode of my story.'

'I shall be here,' replied the man.

And, turning away, he made off.

Ahmed looked at the silver coin in his palm and a tear fell from his half-closed eyelids. Now that he was an old man, he no longer had the strength to hold them back.

That evening, the sky over Ahmed was red: red and blue of a night which, in a few moments, from west to east, would paint Baghdad in those vague hues old women wear in the evening of their lives. The beggar had sat himself down in the same place, there in the great square of the craftsmen's quarter, near one of the gates that closed off the city streets. They said that Harun and Ja'far used to come here in disguise at night and walk in the popular part of the town. Ahmed had followed them only once. When the caliph and his master were together, he would lie on Ja'far's bed and await his return. Always. And Ja'far did return. Always.

He would ask: 'Did you miss me, Ahmed?'

'You know I did master,' he would reply.

'Good,' said Ja'far, 'it is your duty as a servant.'

And then, depending on the day, Ahmed would lie down to sleep at the foot of his master's bed, or in front of his door.

People were beginning to gather around him, the same eyes, the same ears as the day before. Ahmed looked out for the Persian and nodded a greeting when he caught his eye. The man's family, like his fall, must have been great, for his countenance was that of a prince and his clothes those of a pauper. So many noblemen in Baghdad had become beggars thus: merchants with the eyes of poets, storytellers, their words as light as the wind, wandering musicians with the fine fingers of courtiers – so many memories in one gesture or look!

In spite of the oppressive heat, Ahmed was cold. He

would have liked to lie down and sleep. Why talk? Did these people understand even the smallest part of his story? And yet, though poor things in themselves, his words must – like clouds, perfumes, like love – carry all the sensations of the world. He spoke.

The summer that year seemed eternal. Was it the beginning of all our lives, or the end? God is great and withholds his secrets. Messengers had told us that Yahya and Harun were still prisoners. Was it then their death that brought this horseman galloping towards our prison of red earth? Or was it our own disappearance from time that he carried with him, stuck to the sweat of his grey horse? His black abaya streamed out behind him in the wind; he had covered his face. We had gone up to the highest terrace and watched him approach. Seeing the rapid stride of the horse and the clothes fluttering furiously as it ran, I was gripped by an expectation akin to hope. This man was bringing us life. Al-Hadi was dead, buried under his own violence and hate. Al-Rashid was to be our caliph, our chief. After its long rest on Yahya's closed fist, the falcon would at last take flight. Harun came forth from his prison and stood motionless, observing the things and people around him – just as a bird, suddenly stripped of its hood, stands aghast on its master's hand. Suddenly, the world reels before you: freedom and the azure, the rolling of the wind and the warmth of the sun, moment of absolute intoxication before the hunt, before violence and death.

Fadl left straight away to join his foster brother in Baghdad, the brother born of the same hopes as himself, the other half of the golden fruit. We took to the road with our servants a few days later: exiled with us, they would now share the gardens of our happiness. Among them, the Afghan woman, her eyes lowered, refusing to exchange the merest glance with me.

Slow journey in the torrid heat of summer. Approaching Baghdad, we left the convoy and galloped ahead to the round city. There, at the end of the journey, we beheld the same dazzling vision.

'God is great,' said Ja'far simply as he passed through the eastern gate of the outer ramparts. And when the call of the muezzins for evening prayer echoed all around, we bowed down in the dust between the two walls. I shall never forget that prayer. Ja'far took the earth of Baghdad in his right hand and passed it across his lips: ablution or kiss, stain to be wiped away or a pleasure anticipated? He rose, his eyes were clouded as they were just after making love.

'Let us go,' he said, 'my father is waiting for us.'

Fadl was there, standing straight beside his father. I drew aside. Would he even notice that I had disappeared? That same night, it was all made clear to me: the death decided for Yahya and Harun, the execution that was to have taken place the very day of the caliph's assassination. Al-Khayzuran, forced to make a rapid choice, had decided: immediate death for one of her sons and, for the other, the chance to live and reign – the exchange was as quick as a magician's trick. Harun was duty-bound to be grateful and docile, Yahya and she would lead him as their own destiny dictated.

That night, Ja'far did not come. I grew pensive. My master's future rested entirely on my own self-efface-ment: after its slow maturation in the obscurity that was my life, it would at last burst forth into the light, tearing me apart in its wake. From now on, I was too small to keep him, I could only follow him with my eyes and open my arms to him when he came to me – never ask

23

for anything and thus never be refused; simply stay and wait with immobile, mineral strength. I was a stone under Ja'far's feet, a stone bedded in the country of my memories.

Long were the days that followed and short the hours. Yahya and the queen were turning to face their destiny; Fadl and Harun, invisible, were preparing to come out into the broad daylight, and Ja'far now knew that his place was at their sides. How? He knew.

The summer was coiled in the zenith of the heavens and a damp heat weighed on the streets and houses, on the mud bricks baked by the sun; a heat like today's on houses just like these. It was in such an oven, sealed within the roundness of the town, that the caliphate of Harun and the splendour of the Barmakids were being prepared. For seventeen years, a moment of magnificence, a sudden flash of light in the Baghdad sky, would illuminate the three-walled town and spread from the capital throughout the entire Abbasid empire. Seventeen years, the end of the first age of life and passage to adulthood, or the end of the last, bringer of death. People of Baghdad, only you can judge; my good sense left me when my master died.

The community was to make the oath of allegiance, the bay'a, on Friday, after the great prayer. Every quarter was in turmoil. That evening, on this very square, the crowd was so dense that the stars in the sky seemed sparse. Everywhere, cakes were baking, sheep were being roasted and spices and aromatic herbs crushed to powder. Strangers talked freely to each other while those already acquainted seemed transported out of themselves. Everywhere the sound of women's laughter filled the air and children ran from their houses to the suq, knocking into old men and turbaned dignitaries. Gold was passed around and smiles froze as hands clenched abruptly on the coveted coin. Not before many moons will such wealth pour forth in Baghdad again.

In the palace, everyone was getting ready. Can my tongue tell what my eyes saw? Will you yourselves be capable of bringing together in your imaginations the gold, the purple, the madder, the black and the white, the jewels and the embroidery, the music, the perfumes, the sweet and the sour, the Beduins – emirs for an hour before returning to the wind of their dreams – and our imam, Harun, twenty years old and triumphing in his new-found power amid these silk-gowned camel drivers, these steadfast warriors in their long, gold-braided black robes, their fierce expressions and their obedient bearing? Dream, forgetful people, and remember your dream tomorrow: life is a dream and we refuse to sleep. Close your eyes and you will see the mosque, the great mosque, on the day when the prayer was said and the oath was made, see the chandeliers, the rugs, the perfumes burning in cups of onyx and jade and brushing against the carved wooden screen of the maqsurah – the only sign of the caliph's presence, for he was hidden from all other men. Ineffable and secret presence like the thought of love in the heart of man, like desire or oblivion, wreaths of smoke rising up towards the dome, shifting and unreal, joining the pale luminosity of the chandeliers on this summer morning, when the oblique rays of sunlight came to expire on the cool blue of the mosaics that drank them in the water of myriad fountains.

Alone in the maqsurah, a golden crown on his head, a sceptre in his hand, the seal ring of the caliph on his finger, and covered in precious stones, Harun, dressed simply in a white woollen coat, the burdah, turned to give thanks or to beseech – or was he pondering his own destiny, and how he might gently steal it from the clenched fists of Yahya the Barmakid and from his mother, the Berber, and take it fully into his own two arms?

The beauty of Ja'far on that day of a thousand marvels cannot be told, your dreams will fall short of it, for he to whom it is given to see beauty on earth is consumed by love and dies. For a long time, the thought of my master has quelled my appetite for life, and the death I shall receive was promised to me on that very Friday in the great mosque of Baghdad.

Harun was the imam, the Prince of the Faithful; Yahya showed him the way and Fadl stood at his side: two shadows, soon to be three, for a single man. Know that from the very outset Fadl tried to persuade himself that his foster brother shared the same ideal of purity, piety and justice as himself. He knew him well, he knew of the light but also of the darkness that dwelt in his friend. The new caliph was certainly pious – audacious too, at times; cultivated, intelligent, but secretive, he was a sensualist, and cruel as only weak men can be. At the age of twenty he had known hatred, prison and the imminence of death; around him, he had seen plots, calumny and assassination. He had been afraid, and if the sight of blood had made him shudder, it had also made his eyes gleam: thrill of red in the black night of a child's dream. Certainly, he loved his mother, his old master, his foster brother, for sure he loved them . . . but only God sees the innermost workings of a man's heart.

Harun, silent and pensive, was listening to Fadl and it was clear to him that the fabrics of their youths were of two different woofs: his own was shimmering and soft, and he loved to caress it and touch it with his lips; Fadl's was rough and grey, the cloth of a traveller setting out on an unending road. One day or another, Ja'far and Harun would surely have to acknowledge each other, and Fadl would suddenly appear lustreless to the caliph. Destiny is but the will of God.

The summer was drawing to a close: in the palace, in the houses, in the streets, everywhere, a new coolness, a new vigour, as if that year the summer would be followed by spring. A young caliph guided by a wise old man, what better could befall the community of the faithful? From the richest to the most humble, all sensed that the calm river of the present would soon be boiling with a new current.

In the palace, it was a time of joy: enchanters and poets, musicians and scholars, all hurried to refresh themselves at this new fountain; Yahya and Fadl surrounded themselves with the finest minds and Harun with the gayest – youths of twenty like himself, their delicate features neatly concealing mighty appetites. The women were beautiful and Harun desired them all: afterwards he would give them to his friends and thus redouble the ardour with which he could talk of them. The queen watched her son with tenderness as he tasted the pleasures of life; the days and nights were too short to give him his due share of responsibilities. He would have time later, much later. After all, he was only twenty.

Then came Ja'far's day. A day blessed or vomited up by God? I do not know; it is because of that day that I stand here before you now in rags, an image of punishment or survivor from happy times.

Autumn had come, with its shorter days and tender warmth. In the garden, roses heavy with the past drooped over basins where they shattered into a thousand fleeting reflections; their petals, rocked by the wind, spoke of love to the women of the harem: women elusive in their hope-filled submission, sumptuous women, devouring like flame, ambitious for the fruit of their womb, firing the flesh and the heart; sultry and wild, a tender and

27

perverse world that watched the roses breathe out their essence on to the Baghdad wind. At the thought of them, my master would draw himself up and I would bend in submission so as not to see the desire I could not share.

Harun had ordered a banquet for his friends; everything had been made ready in one of the gardens, for the night was sweet. The stars were our roof, our walls the rose and laurel bushes; on the ground were dozens of richly coloured carpets, and everywhere lamps with scented oil, birds from Africa and India in cages of cane and wrought iron. Above the cushions of velvet and brocade where the guests would sit was stretched a black canopy embroidered with silver, like a tapestry on the sky, black for the blue of night, silver for the light of the stars; harmony between the universe and the grandeur of the Abbasids.

The door through which the caliph would enter was marked by a translucent veil which shimmered like the mother-of-pearl lining of a shell, now pink, now amber, and now silver, at the whim of the wind. The caliph would be the last to appear, at the moment he chose, and his guests waited in silence. He would sit alone to one side and, if he wished not to be seen, they would let down a hanging in front of him. The hanging was rolled about its two ebony poles, caressing the precious wood with its blackness, quivering sensually in the nocturnal breeze that blew from the west like a Nubian woman in her lover's voluptuous embrace. Concealed behind a panel of tiles and finely worked stucco, the squatting musicians waited motionlessly for the imam to express his will – docile automatons that would play when the order was given. The light that shone on them from the oil lamp above rippled on their white turbans in a dance that was obscene for these indifferent figures who had climbed the wall of time before falling into the caliph's gardens: they were all old, and all of them were blind.

One by one, the guests arrived and went to their places. The fine flower of Arab and Persian youth, sons of the greatest families and the most powerful tribes, their profiles as keen as daggers or soft and tender like summer fruit. Whether tall or slight in stature, dark or light of complexion, all alike had that proud countenance which yields to no man. Simple abayas were worn side by side with sumptuous embroidered kaftans, dagger belts of camel leather and the most dazzling jewels and, on those silk cushions, they looked like falcons perched on flowering bushes. Ja'far was dressed in white: like the Arabs, he wore a white kuffiya fastened about the head by an iggal of gold thread; no jewels; on his feet, gold-embroidered babouches. I too was dressed plainly in white; my head was bare and I stood behind him, ready to serve. Fadl was absent; he was sojourning in the provinces, trying to settle conflicts on the Byzantine frontier. The caliph did not desire war, not yet. Fadl's absence would bring Harun freedom from that ever watchful gaze, from the certitude and conviction that weighed on him, freedom to be himself – a young man of twenty fascinated by the beauty and intelligence of an eighteen-year-old boy, Ja'far al-Barmaki, my master. Ja'far was sitting opposite the door through which the imam was to enter. The moon was shining on his back, making his sapphire-studded dagger sparkle against his white abaya. On the handle of this dagger, rising up on their hind legs, two golden leopards embraced each other. A peacock strutted past, brushing him with its feathers. Ja'far was waiting. I think he knew.

Suddenly, the musicians began to play, their sweet music shivering lightly through the veil over the door. Harun entered. He looked about him; everyone rose and greeted him, their hands on their hearts. Ja'far was the last to rise. How could one fail to see him? Now the caliph was looking. Slowly, his gaze never leaving Harun's, Ja'far deployed the full length of his body; then he bowed. I knew at once that I was witnessing a decisive moment, that the wind had blown on these two beings and would carry them away in its breath. Where to? To a country where I was not. Harun said: 'Come and sit beside me, Ja'far!' All the young men were watching him. Why him? Why now? Ja'far stood up straight, and in the faint moonlight that filtered through the black canopy only his eyes, his mouth, his dagger and the gold cord about his head were clearly visible. Though they were side by side, their eyes never met. Harun's hands were trembling slightly; he was hunched forward, and seemed to be looking at the Persian carpet under his feet.

'I do not know you well enough, Ja'far, and I am sorry for it,' he said at last and, looking up, he met my master's gaze: 'You are not like your brother, may God bless him.'

The servants came in with dishes in copper and glazed clay. With the fragrance of the roses and the sweet water of the fountains mingled the aromas of meats and spices, pigeons in honey, lamb with cinnamon, fish with saffron; a light wind ruffled the veil behind Harun, who was hardly touching his food. Ja'far had taken nothing. The caliph and my master neither looked at each other nor spoke. The other guests whispered and plunged their hands deep into the dishes that had been set before them; the crouching musicians played on, their absent gazes floating over the scene like moonbeams.

Then, all of a sudden, the caliph took a piece of mutton from a dish and proffered it to Ja'far. I was standing behind my master, and was the only one to hear Harun. 'Eat, my brother,' he said, 'for I do desire it.' Ja'far held out his hand, their fingers touched and I knew how strong was the desire that lay curled in the depths of their mingling gazes. I suddenly felt cold and sick. Something like the claws of a wild animal were tearing at my heart. Although erect and still, I saw my own body fold and fall at my feet. Of the two beings that lived in me, only the servant remained alive, and I had to watch the other die without the slightest shudder. Suddenly, the musicians broke off; everything seemed suspended, perfectly silent; the guests had stopped talking and the servants were still; it was a moment of dream; the only sounds were the wind in the rose garden and the lapping of the water in small waves against the side of the blue ceramic basins. Harun and Ja'far were still gazing at each other. Just then, the caliph burst out laughing and clapped his hands: now he knew he was happy. Immediately, the music started up again, the servants resumed their bustling and the guests all spoke out at once – all were possessed by dark desire and open-hearted gaiety. Ja'far too was laughing: he ate and drank, and I watched him.

The banquet went on into the middle of the night. Now the young men were recumbent on the cushions, their eyes bright from the spices and the steaming food. They were handsome and, even though it was late in the night, the heat was intense.

Once again, Harun clapped his hands; the musicians stopped playing and disappeared. New ones immediately took their place, making fast and ardent music. They sang for a few instants to applause from the guests, then, springing forth from all around – from behind the basins, the oleanders and the marble pillars on the patio – the dancers made their entrance. They were young, beautiful, almost naked, and whirled around the caliph's guests to the jangling of the golden jewels that adorned their brows, their wrists and their ankles. Their breasts, arms and necks gave off a strong scent of jasmine and musk; their fleshy lips parted with the rhythm of the dance to reveal brilliant teeth and their kohl-rimmed eyes stared at the men in silent entreaty. The guests had all sat up; from time to time they laughed, but they never spoke. Their desire was so great that it shone like pain in their eyes.

Harun was watching them too; his hands were trembling, his eyes were bright, staring; his fingers, on Ja'far's, seemed to want to impart to my master the sensuality which had seized him at the sight of these girls, to make an offering of it. Harun gestured to one of the dancers, who came and knelt before him. He bent over her, his hands sought her shoulders, her breasts. He was breathing quickly and I could see the sweat glistening on his temples and forehead. The girl, overwhelmed, was absolutely submissive. Harun kissed her and gave her to Ja'far. Then, his eyes fixed on the caliph's, my master gave her a long kiss. 'Take her!' said Harun.

A great shiver ran down Ja'far's body: he had lost his self-possession. With one hand, he drew the dancer to him; with the other he brushed aside the veil over her hips and forced her to kneel. The girl did not move. When Ja'far took her from behind she started, but said nothing. My master's eyes were still riveted to Harun's. Then, the caliph jumped up, took Ja'far's waist and pulled him away from the dancer.

'Come,' he said, 'let us go.'

His voice was so low that I could hardly hear it.

Ja'far was standing, pale in his white abaya.

'Stay here, Ahmed,' he ordered, 'wait for me!'

I did not move. The other guests shared the dancers as the music became an obsessive growling. The sight of these women, offered up to my desire, left me indifferent.

AHMED'S THIRD NIGHT

Ahmed was alone. He had arrived earlier than on other days, and the townspeople had not yet come out for their evening walk. He had slept all day, squatting in the shadow at the foot of a wall. He knew now that he had a long night ahead of him. The failing light fell obliquely between the weave of branches that formed the roof of the suq and made a dance of the dust kicked up by the asses' hooves. Dried earth, heat, flies; a mixture in suspense, waiting for the wind that would not come; an intimate fusion with the light, the smells and the noises that were covered over by the sleep of the town. Reds and golds, blacks and browns tangled under the saffron sun, forms blurred by the heat that renders all things transient and shifting, making the Beduin rise up on his bed to seek in vain the horizon of his desert. The dark gates of the streets were open, releasing the sapphire blue of the sky on to the white streets, like a panel of mosaic between two wings of cedar.

Ahmed pulled his robe up over his head and listened to the silence. All his life he had been waiting for a noise, a footfall, a voice, and now he was waiting for hope to end. His old body no longer thrilled or quivered now, for it had forgotten emotion; and yet this very stillness was a sensation that roused his memory. How could he forget? Ja'far's eyes were now without a face, wandering inside him in an unending gaze. Sometimes, Ahmed saw in them reproach, entreaty or nostalgia, and then he would close his eyes so as to free his master; but he knew that he would never leave him. From now on, his body was Ja'far, this poor body cast into the dust of

Baghdad was the last refuge of his fallen lord. A long time ago, he had been here, on the corner of this square, with Harun, the two of them disguised as merchants. He was laughing and his teeth shone with the same whiteness as his skull, now dried by the wind on the bridge of Baghdad; the same brilliance, the same love, Harun had desired both of them. Flash of the sabre, flash of desire in the caliph's eye – quick, imperative, absolute moments of fusion, brief instants in the day of time.

Ahmed waved a fly from the back of his hand. There, before him, stood the Persian.

'May salvation be yours, old man. Am I then the only person come to hear you tonight?'

'Men are like sand blown by the wind of chance. I shall speak for you.'

'Come to my house,' said the Persian, stepping towards Ahmed, 'do not throw your past to these dogs. I shall find men who will drink in your words like milk. The Barmakids will live again in our midst, and for us alone.'

'The Barmakids are dead, my friend. My voice is all I have left; leave it with me until I die.'

'For whom, for what, old man?'

Ahmed rose and wiped his face with the edge of his robe.

'For the people of Baghdad, and so that Ja'far may come back here for ever. His true place is here and it is my task to bring him from his lost palace to the humble houses that remain here. Where there is life, there my master is too.'

Already, a few people were gathering around Ahmed. The Persian hesitated, turned his back and left. The old man knew he would never see him again. Another person gone. So, he was then destined to remain alone in Ja'far's embrace; for ever, indivisibly.

The children were sitting, the men remained standing, a few veiled women stopped for a moment; he saw only that their eyes were troubled by the memory of the dead man whom they all had loved. Could the oldest among them remember that body, that face, that smile? Did they understand such beauty? Children are the first to sense the coming fragrance of jasmine in spring, even before it has blossomed; they know its scent. And when its fragrance hangs heavy in the air, even then is it ready to die.

And so it was [said Ahmed] that the splendours of the Barmakids began their reign. All was ordained by them and for them, Baghdad became a diadem laid on their brow, and each of its stones was a gift of love. The weakness of the caliph and his subjects gave the Persians power and pride. But did you know that love is always changing hands and that the last person to hold it invariably gets his fingers burnt? Ja'far died because of his own assurance.

When he understood this, Fadl knew that it was too late, that the esteem in which the caliph held him was hampering his love for Ja'far: he decided to guide Harun from afar, not to impose himself but to be there always. He watched his brother with pity rather than envy, sensing no doubt that Ja'far's position was more fragile than his own, his brilliance more ephemeral. Ja'far dwelt in the body and desires, Fadl in the soul of the caliph – in his better self. Would the family's glory survive their master's passion? He didn't think he knew the answer but, from time to time, his severe countenance wore the fragile veil of disenchantment.

The year went by in gentleness and confidence. Yahya and his two sons dominated Baghdad with their power.

They found land by the river to build their palace. No architect could invent forms pure enough or discover materials noble enough; others were summoned from the edges of the empire. The residence of the Barmakids must be a lake mirroring the glory of the world, itself a pale reflection of their splendour. Walls rose up and green cupolas stood out between the grey clouds of the wintering town; apartments and salons, kitchens and stables, growing endlessly outwards.

Clustering round the fountains in the gardens, rose and laurel bushes formed gracious ranks along marble alleyways. The blue of the ceramics – the colour of Persia – was set like a jewel in the white stucco of the walls in the corridors and courtyards and, in the patios, mosaics filled the pink marble floor with a proliferating life of entwining birds and flowers. The ceilings of carved cedarwood looked down on the velvety fire of the carpets. Cushions and sofas of silver and gold brocade presented their gentle curves as if their very softness could drive out the thought of the vanity that had created them. The palace of the Barmakids was finished for the first celebrations of spring. Dressed in black like a Beduin in his goathair tent, Ja'far received the caliph there, and the caliph saw no one but him, drank only the milk from his eyes and the honey from his mouth. Yahya and Fadl, adulated like princes, contemplated it all with serenity; I myself was but eyes and ears; I did not judge.

Often, at night, when my master was with the caliph, I would roam through the rooms and corridors; the darkness made their huge dimensions even more imposing. There were always some herbs smouldering at the bottom of a perfume burner and their smell slipped into the shadows like a hand. I would follow it to the garden where it embraced the fragrance of the flowers; then, sometimes, I would sit on the edge of a basin and look into the water. I saw there a face that was still young and beautiful, but unloved now: my fingers would caress it to try and make it believe in tenderness, but it did not quiver and my lips themselves stayed closed. I let my hand drop back into the water; like me, it was cold and still – a friend, a sister. I wanted to dissolve into it so that my two images would become one . . . I lifted my fingers from the pool and drew them over my cheeks, my mouth, my eyes, to give them new life, but only the eyes would sometimes respond. Who among us has never cried?

Ahmed fell silent; his voice was trembling, he was tired. Before his eyes, the crowd became blurred, indistinct; even the children close to him had taken on the shifting volatility of clouds. All these people vanished then re-appeared as the water filled and then dropped from his eyes – small, fragile boats on the waves of his memory. How sweet it would be to give himself up to the current of his love, to be rocked by it before slowly sinking for ever. Ahmed raised himself up; this was not the moment, not yet. He wiped his eyes on his robe, grey with a whole age of poverty, and, once again, there they all were – clear, precise, full of blame or praise, severe or kind-hearted, all these people listening to Ahmed's tale.

Ja'far's apartments were as my own: I lived there and slept there; I listened out for the slightest noise, the slightest footfall. Utterly alone, I refused to talk to the other servants or with the women. I prepared for Ja'far a couch where he never lay, meals he never ate, dreams he never shared. He was elsewhere – in the palace, in the provinces, with the armies; where Harun was, there he would be too. Yahya and Fadl ruled, and the Abbasid empire grew and grew.

I remember Ja'far's laugh, his bright eyes when he returned. He was happy, he had everything – honours, wealth, beauty, intelligence, and the caliph's love. He dreamt of a life of grandeur, and his *élan* carried him so high he thought he was a bird. Ja'far wanted everything and everything was possible; in the palm of his hand he held the gold dust of all dreams, the dust which intoxicates and blinds, and which also obliterates the mirages at the end of the traveller's journey. Tenderness and passion, the bonds uniting Ja'far to Harun were made of feathers and lead, and he would laugh whenever he thought of them; those binding me to my master were tied around my own wrists, and only mine, and they made me weep. But perhaps it was only the sand that runs with the desert wind, or the sun, that inflamed my eyes, or the glaring light of noon which dried my mouth and closed my eyes so that I might dream more intensely of the coolness of spring water and April nights. At times I just wanted to saddle my horse and ride into the distance, to gallop for ever in the red dust, caressed by the endless skies of the Baghdad summer. Perhaps then, at the journey's end, I would find peace, an oasis of dates and milk where I could lie down and rise no more, curled up in the sweetness of rest as in my mother's arms, so long ago.

Tambourines and flutes, the panting voice of a young girl; I desired a future that would help me forget my memories. And then, right in front of me – Ja'far; my urge to be one with him, my self-effacement and forsaking of my own desires to be but the reflection of his: love? Call it what you will, words no longer matter.

Look around at the clay ramparts encircling you and lift up your eyes to the dome of the caliph's palace: dust and marble, parched mud and precious metal; you are but the eyes of life, but I have lived. All this will disappear one day, blown away by the desert wind and the gallop of the horses of those who will come from the north. Your bones will bleach in the four corners of the cemeteries of oblivion, and, when God's peace returns, the shadow of Ja'far will spread like a palm tree dispensing coolness and rest. Beauty abides for ever.

At that time, Ja'far began to dream of a palace of his own. The Barmakids had already annexed the western part of Baghdad: there stood Yahya's residence, the Ksar al-Tin, a marvel all in blue and ochre whose rounded cupolas were reflected in the grey waters of the Tigris, near the Basrah gate. Ja'far desired his palace as one desires a woman, with exaltation. A more lavish life was inconceivable, but I knew that he desired above all to separate his home from his father and brother's, to mark his independence and the special status conferred upon him by Harun's passion. Do you remember the pride and insolence of Fadl? Affability and modesty, compared to the arrogance of my master. Ja'far looked through other men with eyes like a bird of prey. Occasionally, his look would settle on me and, with it, his tenderness, and some infinite fragility that made me tremble.

Once again, we watched the arrival, one after another, of carpenters, masons and craftsmen from every corner of the empire. Gold flowed from one hand to another as if from some inexhaustible spring: Ja'far, already so generous, was becoming prodigal. So as to be worthy of the caliph's affection, he desired to build pure beauty on earth. Every part of his palace was a word of love. We saw clay walls raised, doors arched, colonnades of marble enlaced with volutes and cedarwood ceilings along which ran verses from the Qur'an. Then craftsmen came to assemble the mosaics, piece by piece – on the patio walls, where white roses with hearts of jade bent to blue Persian birds with turquoise beaks, and on the fountains which opened like corollas around the black marble dolphins with emerald eyes. In each stone a new flower was framed in colours so brilliant that the sky seemed to bend to Ja'far's palace to see them.

God was with him.

And, set in this magnificent casket of jewels, my master's room was of an extraordinary simplicity, like the tent of a Beduin, forever on the move. A few rugs, a bed, cushions of blue and gold. Above the cedar-framed door, the first verse of a poem, written in Persian:

See, in the country, the mountain gazelle, how it runs!
It has no friends, how can it live without companions?

Opposite the poem, a great mirror repeated the words into infinity, just as it reflected Ja'far's face when, leaving the caliph's chamber, and free of his court clothes, he ran his hands over his face – movement of caress, ablution, purification. One night, one night only, Harun came to Ja'far. When I came in with some fruit and wine, I saw the caliph reading the Persian poem.

'Was there nothing that could satisfy you in Arabic, Ja'far?'

My master, who was standing, bowed.

'Imam, poetry has no country.'

Harun stared at him, and his expression was extra-ordinarily severe.

'It displeases me, Ja'far, when people assert their difference from myself and my race.'

Ja'far knelt down before the caliph. It was the first time I had seen him bow before any man. For a few moments, Harun left him on the ground with his head bowed and did not look at him. Then, slowly, he reached out his hand and touched his friend's shoulder.

At that moment, something extraordinary happened. As he touched Ja'far's body, Harun's expression was immediately transformed and his harsh eyes became troubled, almost imploring. Ja'far raised his head and there followed a long moment of mutual absorption as their eyes met. My master was calm, distant; the corner of the caliph's mouth, and his hand, began to tremble. I could see the power my master had over him and left the room.

They stayed together all night. In the morning, when I came with dates and milk, I saw the submission in the caliph's eyes. It frightened me. Harun went out and, before going to sleep, Ja'far said: 'The caliph is getting married. He is marrying an Arab princess, princess Zubaydah. There will be celebrations that no one shall forget. Zubaydah is the granddaughter of Al-Mansur.'

'Are you worried, my lord, are you afraid of this Arab princess?'

Ja'far began to laugh. His teeth were pointed like a jackal's.

'I have Harun in the palm of my hand.'

He cupped his hand, contemplated it and, with an expansive gesture, stretched out on the bed.

'I am tired, Ahmed, give me a massage.'

I ran my fingers over his back, his belly, his thighs. When he stopped moving, I knew that Ja'far had fallen asleep.

Harun and Zubaydah's marriage celebrations lasted seven days. In the garden, black tents with gold brocade had been pitched by the guests. Under the black flag of the Abbasids, fluttering from a silver canopy woven with gold, Harun sat in the company of the princes, the religious leaders, Yahya, Fadl and Ja'far. The caliph and his intimates ate and drank from gold, his guests from silver. All around were pink rose bushes and white lilacs whose sensual fragrance married that of the spices and burning perfumes; the fiancée too was burning, upright and pallid behind the gold-pearled veil. Only once, on the last day of the celebrations, did she find herself opposite Ja'far, and her eyes, all that could be seen of her veiled face, stared at him defiantly. My master withstood her stare and smiled. Did she see the irony? From that moment onwards, she would never again meet his gaze, and the hatred she conceived for him would never die.

To the sobbing of flutes and the beat of tambourines, each desert jewel was a milestone on the caliph's road to power. The caravans stopped and the camel drivers turned to Baghdad, the goal and reason of every journey. Thoughts of the marriage feast lit up the eyes of merchants and filled the dreams of the young girls behind the mashrabiyahs. They laughed behind their brown hands and boys stopped in the street. So many promises and so much happiness behind such high walls! The impossible within arm's reach and the heat weighing down on all things, ardent to the point of pain. That night, Harun would go to bed with Zubaydah: bejewelled, massaged and manicured, she was ready to be offered up. That night, Ja'far would remain alone.

He had his back to me as he stood before the mirror in his bedroom. I asked: 'Does my master need me?' Ja'far turned round. He was pale, but perhaps that was the fatigue of the celebrations. Would he ask me to stay? My heart was leaping in my breast.

'Go and fetch me the Afghan,' he said, looking into my eyes. I looked down. Never again would Ja'far see me cry. I backed out of the room. The palace harem was on the other side of the gardens. I crossed them slowly.

Why that woman? What could she give my master that I couldn't? The rose bushes caressed me with their sweetness and the mouths of the black marble dolphins wept, their emerald eyes staring at me blankly through the transparency of their unseeing pupils. I sat down for an instant and drank. My throat thirsted for every sweetness and tenderness.

The eunuchs of the harem were dressed in black and blue: they greeted me.

'My master wants Amina, the Afghan.'

They bowed; their faces were inexpressive, living statues beyond time. It was late in the night and the women were sleeping. I waited. Moment of peace as I squatted at the foot of a column in the tepid heat of the patio; the distant song of a girl made me close my eyes. Was it a plea or a song of gratitude? Amina was standing there before me in a long embroidered purple dress, her veil held by two ruby brooches, gifts from Ja'far. Her triumph proclaimed itself in her every gesture and look, but I despised her too much to suffer.

Ja'far was reclining on some cushions, waiting for her. He raised himself up on one elbow and beckoned to Amina to come forward. He gave no greeting.

'Take off your clothes!'

Amina unbuttoned her dress and let her veil fall. Like some nocturnal snake, the shadows and light from the lamp stroked her perfectly smooth amber body. About each of her wrists and ankles was a golden chain. I turned to leave.

'Stay, Ahmed,' ordered Ja'far, 'you are going to see how you screw a girl.'

Amina went up to Ja'far, knelt, and took one of his hands. She kissed it.

'Let him go, master, don't amuse yourself at his expense; he is your faithful servant!'

43

Ja'far looked at me. With our eyes we loved each other more than we ever could with our mouths. He made a sign and I left.

This was the night Ja'far's daughter was conceived, the very night that Al-Amin, the crown prince, son of Harun al-Rashid and Zubaydah, was begotten.

For a few instants, a cloud veiled the moon, which had been beaming down on Ahmed's head, and he fell silent. Without its milky light, the great square suddenly seemed mysterious and menacing. Since Ja'far's death, Ahmed had feared the darkness of night. The wind rose, gently blowing the dust between the merchants' stalls. Here and there, a few braziers gleamed, projecting their play of shadows and light into the wind. Covering their mouths with their gowns, the people dispersed. And thus ended Ahmed's third night.

AHMED'S FOURTH NIGHT

How long had Ahmed been on the square when the passers-by began to gather round? It was as if he had been squatting there for ever on the hard earth at the foot of the brick wall; since the day before or perhaps even longer. Had he slept? No sooner had his mind grasped the present than forgetfulness effaced it, just as, in the desert, the wind erases the dunes, shifting and swelling and flattening them. Since Ja'far's death, Ahmed had no more memories. He would eat whatever a merchant might on occasion give him, drink at the fountain and pray wherever he found himself, turning towards the south. Sometimes, he would speak aloud to himself – broken sentences without a sequel that could be gathered together only at night. Then, raising himself up before his listeners, he would tell his tale.

Harun spent only two nights with Zubaydah, then returned to Ja'far who, half kneeling before him, kissed the edge of his robe. The caliph raised him up and life resumed its usual course. Occasionally, Harun would call his already-pregnant queen, or one of his concubines, to his side; then Ja'far would spend the night with the Afghan or another woman, but most often with Amina, whose breasts were growing heavy and whose belly was swelling. The two men would leave each other only to be more perfectly reunited, for Harun could not go more than two nights without my master. Their relationship was different from those they had with women, more gratifying, for they esteemed and admired

45

each other – and this even though the caliph was dominated by Ja'far. They shared everything – pleasure, study, work, even their thoughts – and their days were spent in conversation and laughter, in political decisions and prayers and quivering delight.

In Ja'far's palace, at the bottom of the gardens, at the foot of the outer wall, was the falcon house. Ja'far went there every day to watch his falcons being trained. He personally chose those birds that combined both aggressiveness and obedience, those that quivered with anger yet would return when called to settle on the falconer's fist.

The understanding between Tarek and Ja'far was immediate and complete. Tarek was a white bird speckled with grey. He and his master were kindred spirits: young, ardent and obedient. They both quivered when they touched, and the call of Ja'far's voice was for the bird an imperative summons. Ja'far himself trained Tarek each morning, and each evening he would gently stroke the falcon's feathers, making sounds in his throat that the bird understood. Friendship, mutual esteem. One day, Ja'far took the falcon out of the town to teach him space, the dimension of the sky against the ochre infinity of the stony earth. The bird trembled with pleasure on his gloved fist. I followed Ja'far. We were alone. The sinking sun stretched our shadows into long black puddles that the earth was unable to absorb. In the golden light, mounted on his horse, with his falcon on his fist, Ja'far looked like some mythical being, God's own dream of beauty made flesh. His light kuffiya encircled his olive-coloured skin, his black eyes, his straight nose, his sensual mouth, his brilliant teeth; he was laughing; he took my hand, he was happy.

When we reached the plain, so far from the town that its ramparts were barely discernible, Ja'far reined in his horse. Side by side, we scrutinised the long stony dunes, this land of shadows – orange, yellow and brown. Game, we needed game. At last, I spotted a palm squirrel scurrying out of some thorny bush and heading for the nearest shelter. Ja'far and his horse were perfectly still; he had seen the animal. With one precise gesture, he removed Tarek's leather hood – a simple hood, without ornament or aigrette. The leash still tied Tarek to his arm. The clasp clicked drily as he released it. I was stock still. The falcon blinked and looked around him, tilting its head as it did so.

'Go, Tarek,' said Ja'far, 'go my lovely!'

And he accompanied the bird with a great sweep of his arm as it took flight. Spreading his wings, Tarek soared and turned. He had seen the squirrel.

Ja'far and I remained motionless. Our horses were touching and Ja'far had taken my hand.

'He'll get him, master. The squirrel hasn't got a chance against Tarek.'

Sensing the danger, the squirrel suddenly turned and ran to the left; still circling, the bird was now slowly descending. Once more, the animal changed course, ran to the right, then again to the left. Ja'far was squeezing my hand. I could see his perfect profile attentive, with not a muscle in his face moving. At last, Tarek, as if in punishment, swooped on his prey. His talons gashed its sides and his beak went for its eyes. Already, the squirrel had stopped moving. Then Ja'far, spurring his horse, brought it up to the falcon.

'Fist, Tarek!' he commanded.

The falcon raised its head in astonishment. The blood spurting from his prey was spattering his feathers, as if with a mask of garnets.

'Fist, Tarek!' repeated Ja'far.

And, opening its wings, the bird came to settle on his

master's glove. Then Ja'far smiled and turned to me.

'Did you see this falcon, Ahmed, did you see him? He is hunting for the first time and he still releases his prey to obey me. Give him his reward.'

I took a piece of raw meat out of a bag and the falcon seized it with one stab of his beak. Ja'far then put back the hood and, caressed by a wind that was sweet with thyme and wild cumin, we walked our horses back to Baghdad under a sky of honey and amber.

'Tomorrow,' said Ja'far, spurring his horse into a gallop as we neared the ramparts, 'tomorrow we go hunting with the caliph. Then we shall see if his falcons are a match for Tarek.'

Thereupon, with his bird still on his fist, he let out a wild yell and set off at full gallop on his white horse towards the Kufa gate.

Rather than follow him, I preferred to watch him fly towards the clay ramparts. The image of his white silhouette against the hemp-coloured walls was to me like a hint of eternity. Mansuetude and violence, perfect clarity and total ambiguity: Ja'far.

From dawn next morning, an unwonted activity reigned in the falcon house. The birds were being prepared for the caliph's hunt. Excited by the noise, the falcons were turning their heads from side to side and flapping their wings. Embroidered hoods, aigrettes and sculpted perches were being prepared. A servant was filling a satchel with strips of raw meat, reward for the birds, and the smell of blood made the predators, who had not been fed for twenty hours, hop excitedly on their perches. Even though it was still early, the atmosphere in the falcon house was already hot and pungent.

Ja'far entered in boots and hunting costume. Over his pantaloons, his blue shirt was gathered in at the waist by an embossed leather belt from which hung a chiselled golden dagger, a hunting dagger unadorned with precious stones. Around his head, a turban of the same blue as his tunic, also without jewels. He had come to prepare Tarek for the hunt himself. The falcon recognised him and hopped eagerly on its perch. 'Beautiful Tarek,' said Ja'far. He went up to the bird, which tried to jump on to his fist. A servant held out a glove and my master slipped it on. The falcon relaxed its talons and sank them into the protective leather. He opened his wings and flapped them excitedly.

'Be calm, Tarek, calm, my handsome bird,' said Ja'far again, 'soon you will be able to show the caliph what you can do.'

Outside, the horses were being saddled; Ja'far was to meet Harun in front of the caliph's palace. A crowd of servants had squeezed into the yard in front of the falcon house; with his falcon on his wrist, Ja'far's tall form was framed by the cedarwood door with its carvings of birds of prey.

'Come, let us mount,' he said, 'we must not keep the caliph waiting!'

Tarek was wearing a blue velvet hood edged with pearls from which rose an aigrette of hummingbird feathers. A blue leather leash with gold studs was tied to one foot. A servant came forward, leading by its bridle Ja'far's white horse with its saddle of blue velvet and gold brocade. It was a pure thoroughbred, spirited and headstrong, pliant only to the hand of its master. I had tried to mount it once, and it had thrown me immediately.

We mounted and set off. Ja'far rode at the head, and I was beside him. Our hunting companions followed, their falcons on their fists, and the servants brought up the rear. We left the palace. In the town streets, the people stepped aside and wide-eyed children jostled each other:

49

everyone admired the birds, the horses and the riders. Behind latticed windows, the women stared at Ja'far and found his beauty equal to its legend. Ja'far looked at no one. Upright on his horse, his falcon on his wrist, he was dreaming: perhaps he was thinking that he did not belong to this class of men and that he would not share its destiny. Slow trot of the horses, chiaroscuro of the streets with the refreshing shade of their palms, play of light on the mud walls, on the merchants' stalls, waxy colours of the fruits, spices with desert hues and, here and there, the jet of a spring arching from a fountain and bespattering the dust.

We crossed the river where greenish strands reached through the grey of the water. It was late summer and everywhere pebbles protruded like skulls polished by the years in the murky light of tombs. On this same bridge, for more than a year, Ja'far's head was spiked – offered up to the crows, the wind and the sun.

Ahmed fell silent and muttered a prayer. In the crowd, the silence was absolute. The magic of the tale had them hanging on the old man's every word, an age-old magic whose spell had been worked around the braziers in the heart of the desert and on short summer nights under the host of stars. The Arab is a listener, and his dream, born of the word, grows familiar and fecund, itself becomes the bearer of other dreams and other hopes that are passed on from voice to voice, from gesture to gesture, from silence to silence. Thrice, Ahmed bowed to the ground; then he continued.

There before us stood the caliph's residence, the Dar adh Dhaab, the Golden Palace, girt by its high earth walls, and with the green dome of the Kubbat al-Khadra, round like a protective belly; and the golden horseman, like a promise of eternity. Harun came out through the great bronze gate; he was surrounded by his Khurasian guard in their black uniforms and followed by falconers, servants, and a whole crowd of people on foot. They closed the heavy gate and the two companies advanced towards each other. Then, spurring his horse, Ja'far went alone to meet the caliph, his hand on his heart. Face to face, the two men beheld each other: Harun, the smaller of the two, thick-set on his black horse; Ja'far, long and slender on his white steed. The animals snorted and shook their manes; we waited in silence a few steps behind.

'May your morning be guided by goodness, Ja'far,' said the caliph.

'And yours by peace, oh Prince of the Faithful!' Then Harun smiled and so did Ja'far: they had left each other only a few hours earlier and their mixed odours were still on their skin.

'So that is your falcon, Ja'far.'

'This is Tarek,' said Ja'far, and, moving his fist, he made the bird open its wings.

'We are going to see him pitted against Arim. Come my friend!'

Reining round his steed, Ja'far took up his place beside the caliph. I followed behind with Harun's personal slave, a great silent Negro. After us come the guard. As we crossed Baghdad, the Khurasians used their riding crops to beat back any onlookers who came too close. A great cloud of dust billowed up around us. In spite of the slaves who beat the air with great ostrich-feather fans, the flies harassed us constantly in the intense heat. Far away, the sound of tambourines was heard, and a voice began to sing. A wedding, a birth? We continued on our way. The gates of the first rampart were opened and we found ourselves in the space separating the two walls: there, straight beyond the second gate, was the yellow earth, stretching out to infinity, a ruddy carpet under the blue of the sky. A light refreshing breeze was blowing through the scrub. A few goats ran away, driven by two almost naked children. A dog came growling up to the caliph's horse. With one stroke of his sabre, the black slave cut its throat and the animal fell, its body racked by spasms with each escaping wave of blood until, at last, it moved no longer, and the blood spread out around it, black against the red ground.

For a long time we proceeded at a walk. Baghdad was far behind us. Harun was the prisoner of his guard and slaves; he could not talk. From time to time he would look at Ja'far and his expression was far from masterly. Ja'far was still carrying Tarek on his fist, in spite of the bird's weight. He was sitting still as a statue in his saddle. Behind us, a servant carried Arim on an ebony perch. The predator's hood was of black silk trimmed with silver braid. There was a pearl and a small ball of black onyx on each of the feathers in his aigrette. Constantly moving his head, he seemed nervous. Tarek was still.

In the middle of a clump of date palms there flowed a spring that was channelled by wooden pipes. Harun turned to his slave and told him he was thirsty. The Negro quickly dismounted and ran to the fountain. He took some water in a golden cup and brought it to his master. Harun took the receptacle, drank, and offered it to Ja'far. Their hands brushed, their eyes met. Even when drinking, Ja'far did not take his eyes from the caliph's. These two men were mutually dependent, like two blind men who hold on to each other to walk. If one falls, the other thinks he cannot stand, and great is his astonishment when he realises that he can go forward alone.

At last, we arrived in the hollow where we desired to hunt. Around us, bare hills, tufts of dry grass, parched thick-fleshed plants and rocks, pebbles, gravel; a super-fine dust that stuck to our mouths and our eyes, and to the hair of our horses. A wind had risen, a hot dry wind from the south, from Arabia, the land to which we all turned five times a day, as towards a promise. The falcons were restless; Tarek himself was moving his head and spreading his wings. He could sense the imminence of flight, of the hunt, of blood and reward. The horses scraped the ground with their hooves. Surrounded by all this quivering animal life, we grew excited ourselves. On foot, the beaters hammered the ground with long sticks and from their throats came guttural sounds – raucous and violent. The hoods of several young falcons were removed and they soared upwards. Some palm squirrels, some rabbits bolted, a bustard made a lumbering effort to take flight. The predators circled, then swooped; the trainers ran up, snatched their prey and gave them the raw meat. Ja'far and Harun stood to one side, watching. It was not yet time to pit Arim against Tarek. A falconer had tied a silk mantle round the neck of the caliph's bird to protect it from the wind. Ja'far had not covered his. He took a silver perch padded with a blue velvet cushion, put it on his horse's saddle and set his falcon there. At last, a beater came running up to us.

'A gazelle, Prince of the Faithful, a young gazelle!'

Harun and Ja'far both let out cries of joy. They removed their birds' capes and hoods and took them on their fists. The predators quivered, flexing their strong, muscular talons and standing erect in anticipation. A clasp was all that held them back: the moment it clicked, they would soar into flight. With the same raucous clamour, the caliph and my master released their birds; they shot up into the sky, black and grey silhouettes like the cormorants of the waves. Tarek was the first to see the gazelle which, with long, panic-stricken strides, was fleeing southwards – an amber-blond silhouette springing from the red jasper of the earth into the sapphire realm of space. Now Arim too had seen it. His wide circles, higher up than Tarek's, grew tighter as he lost altitude. Tarek was turning but did not descend.

'Arim!' shouted Harun, who was standing in his stirrups now, 'get him Arim!'

Ja'far said nothing; not for one instant did he take his eyes off the flight of his falcon; he was hot, long drops of sweat flowed down from his turban to his temples and the corners of his mouth. I wanted to wipe his face but I knew that I must not move. Harun had put one hand over his eyes and angrily pushed away a slave who was trying to fan him. Arim was directly above the gazelle and was continuing to narrow the orbit of his flight. Tarek was now higher than the other bird, and it seemed to me he had no chance of reaching the prey first. Ja'far was leaning forward in his saddle; but for the momentary quivering of his body, his self-control was perfect. Harun was radiant; he was laughing.

'Go, Arim, go!'

Then, in a flash, Tarek swooped on the gazelle: rapid, impetuous, irresistible, he had embedded his talons deep in the animal's neck and his steely beak was digging for flesh and blood. Harun stood motionless like a black marble statue. Before Ja'far had time to utter a shout of joy, I rode up beside him; I had seen the caliph's expression.

Ja'far heard me without turning his head, without moving a muscle in his face. The sweat – it seemed even more abundant now – continued to stream down his face. With a kick of his heel, he rode his horse up to the gazelle, which was still struggling, slithering now in its own blood. Above, Arim continued to circle: he was waiting, as if he knew; he was the caliph's falcon, his time would come. Ja'far put out his arm.

'Fist, Tarek!' he said curtly.

The bird was plunging its beak into the gazelle's neck, tearing out strips of flesh. It turned its small grey head towards my master, blinked, and went back to its quarry. Harun had come forward; he was only a few paces behind us.

'Tarek!' Ja'far repeated, 'Tarek, get on my fist!'

The bird, now in a frenzy of excitement, was no longer listening. It went on digging its talons deeper and deeper into the neck of its spasm-racked prey. Then Ja'far jumped from his horse and walked up to the predator. Tarek had understood; relaxing his claws, he hopped on to the leather glove, submissive, obedient, waiting for his reward, brushing his feathers against my master's arm. Without so much as looking at him, Ja'far drew his dagger and beheaded the falcon. Its head fell to the ground like fruit blown by the eastern wind, and blood from the slumping, mutilated corpse spurted on to Ja'far's arm. With his free hand he tore the falcon's claws from the leather and threw the bird to the ground. Then, without even a glance at Tarek, he turned his horse towards the caliph.

'A falcon which does not obey is a bad falcon. It does not deserve to hunt.'

Harun was smiling, his expression was at once both joyous and hard, like a fixed mask, haughty and absolute. He was triumphant and the unexampled spectacle of Ja'far's submission filled him with an illusory sense of power. My master did not return his gaze. His back was slightly bowed and I alone saw the tear that dropped from his eyes and mingled with the beads of sweat at the corner of his mouth. For the first time in my life, I saw Ja'far cry, and every fibre in my body cried with him.

Just then, Arim swooped on the gazelle, which was still struggling feebly, and began to dig into the exposed flesh on its neck. The black slave called him and he flew to his perch, took his reward and was hooded.

We returned to Baghdad in silence. When he was in his palace, Ja'far kept me alone with him. He was still silent and I knew he was suffering as much from his pride as from his attachment to the bird he had loved. He had tried to pit himself against the caliph and, having lost, he now knew that his combat was hopeless. I brought him wine and fruit; he refused them. He wanted to sleep outside on the terrace, face up to the sky. In his apartments, motionless in front of the door that gave on to the inner patio, he listened to the bubbling of the fountain; he was running his fingers over an amber necklace, caressing each pearl. It was still early; the sun was beginning to set and its light imbued the mosaics with the trembling life of a living garden.

'Ahmed, recite a poem for me,' he ordered.

I spoke some verses to him, verses about love, not war. Ja'far became calm and, very gently, his face relaxed, grew animated; those words of love, told off like beads, restored his confidence. He knew; a smile came to his lips. What he had lost, he would win back a thousand times over, and so it would go on until the game ended. Then, he would leave the table and leave; here or somewhere else, what did it matter where he went? One thing now was certain: never again would the caliph have the power to make him cry, never. Together, we finished the poem by Abu Nuwas, the Golden Poet, the friend of Ja'far and of the Barmakids. We were sitting on the edge of the blue basin.

He brought me liquor, precious as musk, clear as a tear
gathered by the cheek from two unpainted eyes. Endlessly
the innkeeper slaked my thirst and endlessly I drank in the
company of a maid with dazzling white skin. She sang and
she sang and blame stopped short at the door. Ah, yes, leave
the blame there, for blame drives to drink.

We laughed together.

'Bring me wine,' said Ja'far, 'let us drink!'

The wine was cool and sharp and Ja'far's mouth was moist and sweet. I drew close to him.

'To the health of the caliph, may God grant him protection!'

Ja'far began to laugh. His laughter gave me new life.

'To the health of the caliph, Ahmed, may God give him love and glory and may he give me time, patience and victory.'

There was a noise behind us; we turned round. As he moved, Ja'far spilt some wine on the mosaic floor and the bird depicted there became purple – a bloodstain on its wings, near the neck; just a stain.

'A servant of the caliph is asking to speak to you, master.'

And there, already, stood the man: upright, proud, dressed all in black; we knew him; it was the one who came to tell Ja'far of Harun's desire.

'Our master the caliph wishes to see you, Ja'far ben Yahya.'

Ja'far was still sitting, and was running his hand through the cool water of the basin. He was smiling.

'Tell your master I am tired. The sun was hot today and has made me feverish. I am going to rest.'

The servant bowed, his face showing no surprise, no emotion. He backed out, black shadow against the dazzling whiteness of the walls. I waited a few instants.

'Master, don't you think ... '

Ja'far interrupted me.

'It is good that the caliph should recognise the strength of his desire for me; in the same way, some hours ago, he made me recognise that he was the sovereign and master. When a man examines himself, his eye must be clear of self-indulgence.'

The evening was mild. Ja'far walked in his gardens with some friends and ate alone. Then he went up on to the terrace above his apartments and called for musicians. In the serenity of the summer sky, the melody was like a piercing complaint, the eternal nostalgia for an intensely desired but ever elusive liberty, an unending appeal. Ja'far, resting on one elbow, was deep in thought. The wind was warm and the odours of the town rose like breath; intermittent, heavy, oppressive. Suddenly, from minaret to minaret, short, broken and imperative, came the call to evening prayer: the powerful and piercing voices of the muezzins answered each other, enlacing then ebbing into the coming night, mystical and absolute. Ja'far and I bowed down to the ground. Behind us the musicians had stopped playing and were also saying their prayers. The whole palace, turning to the south, respected God's silence.

It was already late into the night and we were sleeping when Harun's messenger returned. I woke Ja'far, and he took the rolled letter bearing the caliph's seal. What news, what disgrace could this so tardily delivered missive contain? Just a few lines: 'I hope that you will recover and be at my palace tomorrow morning for the Council meeting. May God grant you, my brother, a night of peace.'

Ja'far read the message and dismissed the messenger.

'Tell my lord that I will be with him tomorrow; may God bring him wellbeing and a night of peace.'

There was a smile on Ja'far's face as he slept. I drew close to him and placed my lips on his; he did not even start.

The next day, Harun was waiting for my master in the Council Chamber. He did not rise and gave his hand to be kissed. Ja'far pressed his mouth to it and all was forgotten. Yahya and Fadl were there, as were the caliph's private counsellors, together with a whole crowd of clients, courtiers and supplicants. All of them knew, when Ja'far took his seat beside the caliph, that the flower of their friendship had not yet faded. At the very end of the chamber, one man stared at Ja'far with hatred in his eyes: Fadl al-Rabi, the Syrian enemy of the Barmakids.

After the Council, Harun asked my master to accompany him into the gardens, where he desired to take a walk. Ja'far knew that Harun had not been taken in by the motive given for his absence the night before, and Harun knew that he had given way. However tender it might have been, their behaviour was for me a presage of their future violence. No one could win against the caliph. Harun had put his hand on Ja'far's arm.

'Your absence pained me, Ja'far, and your fever burnt me. I do not like to hear that you are ill.'

'Imam, I could not have borne you seeing me tired. Besides, I wanted to rest so as to be able to devote myself to you entirely this evening. I wanted to give you a long and unforgettable night. I have a gift for you.'

'May I know what it is, Ja'far?'

'Master, allow me to keep my silence. Come with me into Baghdad tonight, and I shall give it to you. It is worthy of you.'

Harun had stopped in front of the rose garden. He turned to my master: as the smaller of the two, he had to raise his head to look into Ja'far's eyes.

'I shall be with you this evening and all night. I shall come to you at dusk, after prayer. Will you recognise me disguised as a merchant?'

'I will always recognise you, master, for I am myself only a part of you; your shadow, your memory, your hope. I myself shall be a simple inhabitant of Baghdad: only two ordinary friends can go where I shall lead you.'

The courtiers who had been following behind now joined them: my master made to leave.

'Ja'far!'

'Yes, lord?'

'May peace be with you. Until this evening then.'

Their eyes met only for an instant, but I knew what they were exchanging in that look. Then Ja'far left.

'What gift have you prepared for the caliph, master?' I asked as we made our way back.

'You shall see it tonight, Ahmed, and even you will be amazed.' He laughed. 'Yes, even you.'

Baghdad night, just like today's but without the fear and distrust. The edifice was intact then and the wind of hatred had not yet blown on it. There were four of us – the caliph, his Sudanese slave, my master and myself; two merchants with their servants, conversing as they strolled through the town. Harun was wearing a kuffiya tied with a black wool aggal, which framed his short brown beard; my master's head was bare. We had been walking for nearly an hour. Harun wanted to see every alley, every market. He stopped in front of every crafts-man's shop and asked questions. Thinking that this short, perfumed man with smooth hands would be a rich customer, young boys followed us vaunting their wares. The Sudanese chased them away with no more than a look. Ja'far, who had already bought some ambergris perfume, stopped in front of a shop where mountains of powder were stored in jars of a bluish glass that masked their colour. An old man squatting behind the stall laughed and pointed to the containers and said something we were unable to understand. Ja'far went up and questioned him, then he too laughed.

'As thanks for the present you are about to receive, give me a little of that powder and I shall make you happy all night long.'

Harun smiled.

'You don't need its help, Ja'far, to make me happy, but let us try it if you so desire.'

And he bought a flask of the yellow powder and passed it to the Sudanese.

'May God bless your beauty,' said the old man, closing his hand over the coins given him by Ja'far, 'when it comes to making the eyes sparkle, it is worth all my powders and all my aphrodisiac talismans put together.'

Harun looked at Ja'far then as one would look at a treasure.

'Where are you taking me, my friend?'

Ja'far put his hand on his shoulder.

'I am taking you to a place of which the memory will set your heart racing. Come.' And the four of us walked through the night towards the Persian jewellers' quarter.

The shop was small and dark; Ja'far knocked on the door. A moment of silence. An ass or mule kicked the wooden door to our left. A night bird screeched. Ja'far knocked again. At last, a small thin man, barefoot in a coarse white cotton robe, came to let us in. He was holding an oil lamp and he was blinking in the weak light. He stared at us and, recognising Ja'far, laid his hand on his heart and tried to kiss the hem of his coat. My master stopped him with a simple gesture. The old man kept repeating: 'What an honour, my lord, what an honour!' He made way for us and we went in. A square room with a floor of beaten earth, a counter draped with an embroidered rug, a chest, two stools; some glasses and a teapot had been placed on a copper tray supported by a three-legged stand. The modest interior of a small tradesman.

'To what do I owe the honour of your visit, master?' said the old man, bowing profusely as he stood before us.

'Is your daughter here, Khalid? My friend would like to see her.'

The little man stepped back, as if trying to protect himself.

'My daughter? My Aziza, lord? You well know that she cannot receive a stranger in her bedroom!'

'Take us to her, Khalid, and you will not regret it: neither you, nor your wife, nor your daughter. You shall have riches and honour.'

'No, my lord, my daughter is so young! She cannot.'

'Khalid,' said Ja'far curtly, 'take us to your daughter; later you will understand and bless me.'

'Very well, my lord,' replied Khalid.

His voice was trembling; raising his hand, he revealed a narrow stairway that led up from behind the counter. Ja'far went first, followed by Harun and his servant. I was the last. In front of a blue-painted wooden door, Khalid stopped.

'It is here, my lord; but she is sleeping.'

'Wake her.'

The father went in alone. A few moments later, the door opened again.

'Come in, my lord – you and your friend; my daughter is waiting for you. Be patient with her, she is so young!'

He put the lamp on the floor and went away. Turning round, I saw a fat, red-haired woman – probably his wife; she seemed terrified. They made off together. Ja'far went in and said a few words to the girl. She was sitting on a narrow bed. Then we all saw her. The beauty of that child was dazzling, incomparable. Harun murmured in admiration.

'Look,' said Ja'far, 'here is my present. Is it not a kingly gift?'

Aziza was staring at us with terror in her eyes. She was fourteen, fifteen perhaps, her hair a deep blonde colour, almost red, and her huge eyes green and golden at the same time. Her nose was small and straight, her mouth full, her teeth fine and regular, extremely white.

'Rise, Aziza,' said Ja'far in a gentle voice, 'do not be afraid: this man means well, he is my friend.'

The young girl stood up. She was tall and slim and through her transparent robe could be seen a perfect body: round thighs, full hips, swelling, pointed breasts, a slim and supple neck. She was trembling, frightened like an animal flushed from cover.

'Take off your dress,' said Harun, 'I want to see you better.'

The young girl shook her head. Ja'far took her hand.

'Obey, Aziza. This man is going to be your master and you could not have a better one.'

Then Aziza lifted her long white shirt over her head and appeared before us, naked in the flickering light of the oil lamp. She was crying and hiding her face with her hands. Harun seemed overwhelmed. Dazzled, he stared at her for a few seconds and then, in a gentle voice, said:

'You can put your clothes back on. From now on you will take your dress off only for me.'

The child obeyed. She had still not uttered a word. Harun went up to her, scarcely daring to touch her.

'You are beautiful, Aziza, and already, I want you for myself alone. You shall never regret this day, I promise you. Dry your tears.'

And, turning to his black slave, in a voice which had once again become dry and authoritarian, he commanded:

'Take her to the palace and have the women prepare her. I want her with me tomorrow night.'

The Sudanese took the young girl by the arm with extraordinary gentleness, as if suddenly his master's happiness was the most precious thing in the world. Aziza was passive, terrified.

Downstairs, the mother and father were waiting for us. They had seen their daughter leave and were lamenting. From his abaya, Ja'far took a heavy-looking leather pouch and gave it to the father.

'This is to repay you for your daughter's services. It is only the beginning. You shall receive much more, for Aziza shall be the companion of the caliph.'

The parents, struck dumb with surprise, flattened themselves against the wall and let us pass. The father had taken the bag of gold and was clutching it to his body.

Out in the street, Harun took Ja'far's arm.

'That child truly is an exceptional gift, Ja'far, and I thank you for her. How did you discover her?'

'Her parents are Persians who have served our family for generations. Aziza's father is a jeweller and from time to time he comes to the palace to propose jewels for my concubines. A few weeks ago, his daughter came with him and I was struck speechless by her beauty. I thought of taking her for myself but decided that only you were worthy of such beauty. I give her to you as a love offering; she will bear you a son and I, Ja'far al-Barmaki, I shall be his tutor, for it was Fadl that queen Zubaydah chose for her child; this one shall be mine.'

I immediately understood that Ja'far was pushing this exceptionally beautiful young Persian girl into the caliph's bed so that his master's heart would henceforth be divided between our race and his own; his affection shared for ever by the two sides. Aziza was Ja'far's answer to Zubaydah, protection for himself and his family.

I was alone with Harun and Ja'far; we returned to the palace. I knew that I would be alone that night, also. Harun would know how to thank my master for this royal gift.

With the Sudanese, I slept before the caliph's door. Ja'far emerged only at dawn. He seemed happy.

Ahmed fell silent and raised his head to look at the human circle surrounding him.

'Go now, leave an old man to his memories: may God grant you a night of peace.'

And, turning their backs, they made off, one by one, into the night.

AHMED'S FIFTH NIGHT

Already, a few clusters of people were standing by the wall where Ahmed was wont to sit. But he was not there. And yet, night had come, and other storytellers were squatting there, making the night wind shiver with their great dreams. Around the braziers, jugglers, snake charmers and magicians were inventing space, adventure and time. The Baghdad sky arrayed its stars about the moon and the moon itself came to contemplate the golden horseman – still, hieratic, luminous against the navy blue of the sky. In large bowls, merchants were cooking mutton, vegetables and spices, which their customers ate standing up in their haste to make their way to the next ephemeral, magical place. Each night, the Arab tongue, so rich with images, so precise, poetic and direct, gave the great square of Baghdad a new life in which anything could happen.

At last, leaning on the arm of a child, walking bent to the ground as if fruit too heavy to bear bent the branch of his old age, Ahmed arrived, and the crowd stepped aside to let him through; they were silent and respectful before this old man, the witness of another age, of another way of loving, of the time when the caliph dwelt in Baghdad and gave her life. The wind and the rains had worn down the ramparts and the palaces; the clay was cracking, letting through the winds from the east and the west; and of Harun's Gold Palace, only the great walls of white marble remained, immuring silence and forgetfulness.

Then Ahmed dropped to the ground; his body, huddled on the earth as if he somehow wanted to sink into himself. The child accompanying him sat beside the old man and, with his head in his hands and his eyes wide open, he listened.

Fadl al-Barmaki had won a great success in the rebellious provinces of Persia. He had obtained the submission of the rebel Yahya ben Abd Allah, the Alid, the hero, his friend since their first meeting, when mutual esteem had united for evermore the chief of the rebels and the family of the Barmakids – lovers of liberty and fiercely partisan when it came to the thoughts and actions of those they admired. Yahya ben Abd Allah was loved in Persia and hated in Baghdad. Fadl al-Rabi, the Syrian, who used every means to insinuate himself into the caliph's intimacy and who hated my master, had aroused Harun to vengeance: blood to wash away blood. Fadl al-Barmaki himself had had long discussions with the caliph about his convictions and Harun, his foster brother, his friend, had trusted him; he had departed and now came back bringing peace and a defeated man who freely retired to Medina, bound by his promise never to fight again.

Harun's prestige spread to the edges of the empire and far beyond: a son, Muhammad al-Amin, was born to him of queen Zubaydah and Fadl was his tutor. Not long before, Leila was born, the son of Ja'far and the Aghan. Ja'far set little store by her and this made Amina bitter; she too wanted to bear her lord a son.

Aziza was pregnant. The beautiful Persian, beloved of the caliph, her goodwill towards my masters like a kind of tenderness, was going to give the community of the believers two caliphs, her sons, and then two more, her grandsons. Harun loved no other woman than her and she loved only him; she was humble before queen

Zubaydah, the Arab princess who was filling Baghdad with the achievements of her power and greatness, and strong before the caliph who cherished her. Baghdad was at peace, fountains flowed in the gardens and at court poets offered men their sovereign tenderness and the music of their thoughts. Ja'far, showered with honours, gave Harun the illusion of immortality: fascinated by my master, he saw himself in his image: beautiful, intelligent, superior, invulnerable. Thus, the simple gift of satisfaction and pleasure made the Barmakids the absolute masters of Baghdad. And yet, little by little, Harun was changing; his piety, always great, was becoming exclusive, and he was beginning to listen more and more to the hate-filled Syrian who, cunningly, gently, instilled into him the idea that he himself could only become the greatest and most powerful sovereign in the world when free of his passion and his attachments, face to face with the God whose representative he was on earth. He never once spoke of the Barmakids, but he pointed to a path of salvation that was much too narrow to accommodate them. The caliph hardly listened to him, but still he heard him. The idea of separation from Ja'far was no longer totally alien to him and, when trouble once more broke out in Syria, Harun asked my master to cover himself with glory there.

We set off. On the eve of our departure, the caliph wept, overwhelmed by this imminent separation. His strength had deserted him. He would have given away his seal for Ja'far's body, his skin, his odour, the softness of his mouth, the strength of his arms. He suggested a substitute, a general who could leave instead of my master, but Ja'far was not the kind of man to discharge himself of a mission on the mere whim of a lover. Besides, his family itself encouraged him to go, believing that this separation from the caliph would bring them greater safety. Fadl had had a son, Al-Abbas, and he wanted to see him grow up in the Ksar al-Tin, the palace of the Barmakids. He believed that, with Ja'far far away, Fadl al-Rabi's hatred would fall flat like a sail without wind.

The troop following my master was immense; the caliph in person accompanied Ja'far beyond the ramparts and, reining round suddenly, galloped back to Baghdad. Ja'far smiled. The route was long. We rode at the head, followed by the caliph's horseback Arab guard and the light guard on tall blond meharis: their uniforms were all black – colour of the Abbasids, colour of vengeance. Then followed the cavalry, the Turkish, Iranian, Afghan, Egyptian and Sudanese mercenaries, the footsoldiers, the servants with all the packs, the chariots, asses and mules loaded with provisions and water. Ja'far had his servants, his dishes, his tent with its rugs and pieces of material, his musicians, and his astrologers. He had asked for nothing but was the prisoner of his nobility and his wealth. He wanted to be free and rode alone. We spoke together of our past, of our shared tastes for poetry and the arts, and of our future. I savoured each instant of my solitude with him.

The days passed; we continued to head west and crossed the Syrian frontier. The horsemen were tired, the infantry covered in mud and dust; we all yearned for rest, and yet we must fight.

Forever receding horizon; we lived in constant expectation of attack yet had no idea where it would come from. Every town we passed through was a trap, fear lay in wait for us at each stopping place. We slept with our faces to the east so as to see better the first light of dawn. The night was hostile. Ja'far spoke to me of Damas; he was looking forward with joy to the first prayer we would utter in the great mosque of the Omayyads, crossing the stone esplanade that shone from centuries of pilgrims until we could see only the minaret behind the mosaic and marble-decorated transept. In the desert we were crossing, each new day brought hope. Since they could not ride far ahead of the column, the meharis and horses advanced slowly under the heat of the sun; it clashed against their impassive certitude. The black Arab warriors rode upright on their steeds; did their eyes see anything? Battle was their only future, and their only memory the blond dunes and the oases where coolness flowed and the wind blew. At night, our giant shadows stretched towards Baghdad: the musicians played in the dark around shifting fires and men sat dreaming with their chins in their hands. The black eyes of women hovered among their fantasies and, with them, laughter and the guttural sound of pleasure in love. Then from their throats there rose a violent and sad threnody that the night echoed back to the four corners of their memory. To Damas, to Damas, if God so willed.

Then, at last, came the liberating combat – ardour and suffering to free men from their dreams and make them forget. Ja'far had wanted to negotiate but was forced to defend himself, and he acquitted himself with great skill. The rebels fled, we burnt the villages where they might hide; purifying fire, peaceful in its brutality: the desert effaced it all.

Strong from this first success, Ja'far wanted to accelerate our progress to Damas so as to meet the governor, the notables and the religious leaders. We left the troops behind us and set off with the cavalry and the meharis. The desert wind swelled the black standards and the dust enshrouded them; flux of the Abbasids' glory and power.

Ja'far was the first to enter Damas: even before proceeding to the governor's palace, he went to pray in the Omayyad mosque. The Arab guard behind protected him, fierce sentinels of a man for whom they had no love – and this on account of no personal hatred, but because their blood was different. The prayer room dazzled us. Ja'far looked around him like a child. Petrified in the mosaic, a fantastic forest stretched out its branches to imaginary towns over which firebirds watched; a whole world freed by the prophet fell into place around the great brass chandeliers, bright as suns. Silence, odours of burnt perfume and cedarwood, penumbra stooping to breathe in the light on the deep red of the carpets, mythical universe wrapping itself like a star round man's idea of God, distant and near, memory or hope of love. Prostrate, an old man was praying, and the light, falling obliquely on to his woollen coat, made him seem both donor and beneficiary of some offering, bearer of a message from the depths of time into the eternity of human solitude. The noises of the world stopped in the vast courtyard of the mosque and, for the first time, Ja'far noticed its silence.

'May peace be with you,' he said to me.

Our eyes met.

'I will never leave you master,' I murmured.

'Tush,' he replied, 'one day, we shall all leave each other.'

And he bent down to pray.

The meal at the palace was sumptuous. Whole sheep roasted in the gardens, and the odour of wood and herbs wafted into the vast hall where the guests lay on silken and velvet cushions. The light from the torches caressed the huge copper trays, where servants in white tunics with blue belts – Ja'far's colour – came to set down the steaming earthenware dishes filled with meats in sauce, vegetables and cereals sprinkled with coriander, cumin, saffron, chili and fresh mint. Accompanied by some musicians, a tall woman was singing the greatness of the

Abbasid caliphs, and her endless chant echoed their eternal glory. The governor was profuse in his promises but each of his smiles, each of the gestures of his chubby, bejewelled hands confirmed to Ja'far that he would be utterly alone. This man was nothing. Unaided, he must pacify this country and impress on its every man, woman and child the vital facts: it was in Baghdad that their sun now rose every morning. Moist with wine and meat fat, the guests' lips shone under the torchlight, and the hands dipping into the bowls, the expressions on each face, the laughter and the silences were like so many signs of low ambition and petty hopes. In their midst, Ja'far was like a pool of pure water in a muddy road. When the dancers entered, Ja'far rose and went out; this, he deemed, was no time for amusement.

We set off at dawn for the north, towards the Zebdani region in the Al Sharbi jebel. There, in the mountains, was the core of resistance; that was where we would have to fight. The temperature was cool at this end of autumn. Ja'far, wrapped in a big woollen coat, was silent; I followed him a few paces behind. He turned around to see the walls of Damas and the minarets of its mosque for one last time; his look was a farewell. We marched for three days. It was cold; the lowering sky, the wind, the arid mountains, the hostile stare of the peasants, and the nervous tension that builds up before an ever-elusive battle – all this gave our mounts a heavy tread and made us hunch our backs. At night, the army leaders sat in circles around great fires that were like bunches of asphodels set in front of a great black wall-hanging; Arabs around one fire, Persians around another. Upright and proud, the Arabs took curdled milk, biscuits and dates. They sang Beduin threnodies about the relentless sun and the long dunes where, as if it were the desert's only running water, it travelled towards an eternal becoming. We dreamt of our rose gardens where fountains murmured; of cool wine served in silver cups and of the first odours of jasmine in the mountains. Isolated in this unknown land, each man rediscovered the vision of his childhood, the tenderness of his first years; a perfume, a light seen at the dawn of life and which sets the heart beating for ever. Staring into the flames, Ja'far recited Abu Nuwas, bringing the happy days spent in Baghdad back to each man's memory.

> *Borrow not pastimes and customs from the Arabs*
> *of the desert.*
> *Theirs is a poor and meagre life!*
> *None of life's refinements is known to them, let them*
> *drink their milk*
> *In a land of thorny shrubs and acacias*
> *Where hyena and wolf are the only game.*
> *Spit if you will in their curdled milk, for it is no sin*
> *Better by far is our pure wine, served with skill*
> *around the table,*
> *Wine long-aged in a barrel, wine that warms yet*
> *shows no flame!*

And we laughed, perhaps to hide our desire to weep. The next morning, the weather was fine and the rays of sun straightened our backs and quickened the pace of our steeds. Walls of mountain rose sheer on each side as we travelled along the gorge. A parched torrent rolled its stones under the hooves of the horses: a few birds of prey were circling high over our heads, level with some lost village perched inaccessibly on a peak above our path; its ochre walls stood out against the soft blue of the sky.

Ja'far pointed at the birds.

'Look, Ahmed, two falcons and a sparrowhawk!'

'Yes, master,' I replied, 'I see them. They are hunting.'

At that very moment, there was a din of savage yelling and stones were rolled into our path, stopping us in our tracks. From all around, men, barefoot, were hurtling down at us, shouting and brandishing daggers and sabres.

Instinctively, we drew together. A few horsemen had followed us, but the Arab guard and the meharis were far behind and we were totally outnumbered; the men kept pouring down from the mountain like a torrent under the autumn rain. Ja'far had drawn his sword: erect in his stirrups, he turned to see how many men he could count on, then, with a long piercing cry, he thrust his horse forward. I tried to stay with him but was constantly having to hack myself free with my sabre. Now on the smooth rock ran rivulets of blood that spread into pools where the horses dipped their hooves. The birds of prey were still circling; I remember raising my head and seeing them. Surrounded by a good ten men, Ja'far was defending himself fiercely. Arab and Persian horsemen together, we had taken shelter behind an enormous rock that jutted out into the gorge. Thus, we could only be attacked from the front. Ja'far stood at our head. 'We must break out of here,' he shouted, 'and turn back. Forward!'

And, from every breast, there rose the supreme invocation.

'God is great, God is greater than all things!'

The attackers, themselves caught in the pass, were finding it difficult to fight; we hacked our way through them leaving in our wake severed heads, hands and arms, scattered like wheat cut at the end of summer. A few horses fell, and the riders were at once surrounded by dozens of rebels and killed. The dust burnt our eyes and the smell of blood made us yell. At last, we managed to reach a hollow that was thick with scraggy trees and thorny tufts. Had the rebels seen that Ja'far was our leader? They rushed in at him in swarms and, in spite of our efforts, we were unable to stop them. I could only go to him and fight at his side in the hope that his life would draw new strength from my own. Suddenly, Sanama, my master's beautiful white stallion, fell to the ground; the blood gushed from his flanks in great pulsations as if his heart were continuing to spend its energy outside him. Ja'far rolled to the ground and picked himself up immediately. Standing with his back against the rock, a dagger in one hand and his sabre in another, he was like a cornered wolf in his tattered abaya. A knife cut into his shoulder and blood began to flow along his arm to his hand before mingling with the dust on the ground. With one leap, I was on the ground beside him.

'Master, take my horse.'

Ja'far did not hear me; I was screaming now.

'Master, there is my horse!'

Ja'far gave me a glance. He had understood. He shook his head:

'Go on Ahmed, save yourself.'

I let out a cry that was like a sob.

'I shall never leave you master. For the love of God, take my horse and fly!'

We were standing side by side; behind us, the surviving horsemen were trying to free us. The dust made everything opaque – or was it the sweat and blood which were clouding our eyes? We could hear the clashing of sabres, the whinnying of horses and the clamour of men.

Then, when I had reconciled myself to dying with my lord, we heard the drawn-out warcry of the camel riders of the Arab guard – that unforgettable, piercing, guttural sound. Ja'far's look met mine.

'The meharis,' he said, 'the caliph's guard!'

With long strides, at full gallop, here came the blond

meharis mounted by the men in black – barefoot men with their heads wrapped in their kuffiyas. The caliph's standard snapped in the wind as they charged. And all of them, brandishing their lances, as if flying on their animals, all of them were rushing towards us and yelling their warcry.

The rebels turned and hesitated a moment, not knowing what to do, then they were overcome with terror. They tried to run away, to climb up the mountainside, to go back to the path we had come down and hide behind the rocks which would block the pass to the meharis. They did not have time. Already, the Arab guard was upon them, running them through from up on their mounts, splitting skulls, piercing necks and shoulders, pursuing the last fighters and stabbing them in the back. A lanky mehara stopped beside Ja'far and its Arab rider took him up in his arms and sat him on its back; he wheeled round and galloped towards the rest of the army; I remounted my horse and followed.

My master was bleeding heavily. The soldier took off his kuffiya and rolled it about his shoulder. He stopped by a stream and I joined them. With the help of the mehara rider, Ja'far had dismounted; I would allow no one other than myself to take care of him.

The hour of vengeance had come. For every dead horseman, a village would burn; all night, the Arab guard and the mercenary foot soldiers, the élite and the scum, would cut throats, burn and rape. They cut off the rebels' heads and set fire to their harvests. Where these mutilated, unremembering corpses lay strewn across the ground, there too lay the rebellion. Because hope and memory were no more, Syria was pacified.

We rested for a few days, then Ja'far decided to go further west, as far as the sea, to make sure that there was no resistance there. I knew that he wanted to see what was at the end of the road, that endless stretch of water he had never seen, the Mediterranean. Village after village, town after town, the chiefs and elders came to us with words of peace. As the envoys of the caliph, we were welcome, the honour of their cities. Their friendly speeches had the whole population on our side, but when we rode down the streets, the people all went into their homes and locked their doors. Behind the ramparts, we left silence. A few children watched us leave, dogs barked after our horses. On our right, the undulating foothills of the mountains that we would skirt in the south; monotony of winter under a grey sky rent now and then by the wind. The rains came and the mud caked on the shoes of our horses and the feet of the infantry. Ja'far was silent. He had had no news from the caliph. Carried by messengers who left every day for Baghdad, my master's long letters had now become brief military reports. Ja'far too had become taciturn: silence against silence; pride against pride. Because one of these two men found himself without strength when he was in the other's presence, they were now confronting each other at a distance, when everything is easier, and more definitive.

We no longer spoke of Harun, but I could see from my master's eyes that he was still in his thoughts.

The countryside was beginning to flatten out and grow verdant; scraggy clumps of trees cracked in the west wind. Astonished and delighted, the inhabitants came running to see us. The smell of bloodshed had not reached these people. The women laughed as they lifted their veils over their faces, the young admired our horses and the children hid at the sight of the meharis. The chiefs came to meet us and offered us their hospitality, meagre meals in poor houses. Did they surmise the grandeur, the riches, the power of my master? Sitting on an old rug, Ja'far ben Yahya al-Barmaki, friend of the caliph, the most feared man in Baghdad, the most envied also, ate beans, fatty mutton and lentils from earthenware plates, his marvellous face dappled with light and shadow in the weak glow of soot candles that smoked and made him cough. Now and then, the young men, the sons or nephews of our host, would steal a look at my master, but he did not see them. He was still dazzled by the brilliance of the caliph's love.

And then, one morning, when the winter sun was at its zenith, we smelt a different odour, we heard a special sound: the grass, short and thick, was trembling in a wind that was both stronger and more gentle, the olive trees were bent eastwards. High brick walls rose up as the imposing ramparts around a town that was hunched up about itself like a shivering bird: the ancient Sidon, beating heart of the antique world, now slumbering behind its fierce towers, towers no longer feared. Like two open arms, the port embraced the sea, drew it to itself, cradled it, rendered it inoffensive and submissive like an amorous panther, its claws drawn in, its mouth foaming, with a quivering backbone where bright-hued boats bobbed up and down. At the end of the town, which we had entered alone, Ja'far now rode his horse up on to the quay; he had not uttered a word. Ships were unloading full wineskins from Cyprus and others were loading olives, vegetables and jars of oil. We rode down to the shore. Ja'far's horse stepped back and stiffened but he prompted it forward with his knees. The beast was now up to its chest in water.

'My lord,' I cried out, 'don't go any further!'

He was not listening to me and continued to advance. The horse shivered and snorted loudly. Again, I called out:

'Master, I beg of you, come back!'

Then Ja'far turned to face me. For one brief moment I thought that he was crying, but it was the wind irritating his eyes – or perhaps the sea spray. He drew his hands over his head like a man waking up.

'One day or another, Ahmed, I shall be swallowed up, perhaps tomorrow, perhaps later, God alone knows; but not today, not yet. I must wait.'

And, making his horse back out of the water, he returned to my side. In silence, we joined the rest of the army. It was time to go back.

Ja'far gave the order to avoid Damas. He wanted no speeches, no meals, no celebrations. All he wanted was to be in Baghdad as quickly as possible. Stiffening at the caliph's silence, refusing to be the first to bend, he had prolonged the expedition, perhaps expecting a letter of recall; it never came. There, before the sea, he had made his decision: since he was lost, he preferred to fight, to return and reconquer Harun while he still had the power, now, as quickly as he could. Behind him he left a detachment of troops: the cavalry, the foot soldiers and the packs. Accompanied by the caliph's Arab guard, we headed east at a forced march. The wind was cold, the air dry. Wrapped up in our woollen coats, with our kuffiyas around our faces, we let ourselves be rocked by the rhythm of the horses, alighting only to give the beasts a few moments' rest and to sleep. I took care of Ja'far's food and his sleeping arrangements. I unrolled his mat for prayer, I pitched his tent, I slept at his side. He did not touch me but would occasionally take my hand, and I kept it until I too succumbed to sleep. In the night, when I awoke, I went out of the tent to look at the winter sky, and then I returned to see my sleeping master. God had given the world many beauties.

We were now crossing the Syrian desert. The nights were cold but, in the daytime, the sun allowed us to cast off our coats and let down our kuffiyas. Birds of prey flew high above our heads: silence and peace rode with us, gradually eroding Ja'far's anxiety and gravity and, from time to time, bringing a childlike expression to the faces of the mehari riders. When we came to vegetation, we hunted a few gazelles. We roasted them, and my master ate them with the leaders of the guard. They laughed. Around a camp fire, there always comes a time for legendary tales and, under the Syrian stars, Arabs and Persians together, we heard about the warlike exploits of men's fathers and about their own feats too. Then came the moment for tales of love and the triumphant voices grew nostalgic. Their loved ones were far away, and far away was the breath of their mouths, the heat of their bodies. Though hidden in the sobriety of words, their desire and their longing were great. Around us, a few jackals howled and the wind made the fires flicker as men's voices and hands trembled with the memory of a breast or the perfume of a head of hair.

We were in Iraq. At the sight of the first village we shouted for joy; hope made us straighten in our saddles and quickened the pace of our horses. Outside the town of Kasr Amidj, at the foot of the fortifications, we were joined by a horseman. He had a message from Yahya al-Barmaki to his son; news of our return had already reached the capital.

'Read it,' said my master.

He had just become acquainted with the contents of the letter and his expression had frozen.

Yahya informed Ja'far that the caliph had left Baghdad for the fortified town of Raqqa, in the north of the country. The official reason was to be nearer the Byzantine frontier, a constantly troubled region, so as to wage the holy war with greater ease. He had gone there alone with Fadl al-Rabi, leaving Baghdad to the

Barmakids, leaving the power in Yahya's own hands. He did not seem to be hostile to their family, not yet, and still listened willingly to Fadl, Yahya's son, who had gone to be with him in his new residence. Great now was Harun's piety: he denounced the impure, the luke-warm, all those who in any way infringed the Prophet's law. Yahya was worried at his intolerance. Fadl al-Barmaki, the friend of the Shiites, a tolerant and lettered man, still hoped that the caliph would resist becoming a tyrant; not him, not his foster brother – he was badly advised, he would realise where his true greatness lay.

Yahya beseeched Ja'far to return as quickly as possible: he must recover Harun's friendship, make him give up his excessively narrow views and think instead of extending the caliphate's influence throughout the empire; he must make him agree to return to Baghdad. Ja'far could still do this; he, his father, was sure of it. He had not raised Harun himself without coming to know the depths of his heart. Yahya ended his message with these words of hope: 'They say that the caliph will be in Baghdad for your return, that he is already on his way. Do not delay. May God give you salvation and peace, my son, and bring you back to our side.'

I gave Ja'far the letter.

'Nothing is yet lost, master. The caliph will return to us as soon as he sees you, I know it.'

'May God heed your words,' replied Ja'far, 'and come to my aid.' He stood still for a moment with the message in his hands, his eyes lowered: suddenly, looking up he said:

'I shall not survive if Harun abandons me. Of all the beings in this world, he is the closest to my heart.'

His eyes had glazed over. It was the first time he had spoken to me like this of his feelings for the caliph. I replied softly:

'I know, master, I understand perfectly what you mean.'
Ja'far smiled:

'Let us go now; in a few days we must be in Baghdad.'

We did not go into the town and continued our march eastwards.

The child sitting beside Ahmed had not moved; holding his head in his hands, he was travelling beyond words, beyond the tale, towards a fabulous and magical world of the imagination where his own life was transformed and burst open to the four horizons of an impossible hope. When, on the great square of Baghdad, the hour of storytelling came, all men alike were reborn into a new life, a life hidden in the long monotony of days. Beggars became princes, craftsmen kings; in a twinkling, each working person became the grand vizier of the night, and all things were as ordained by him and for him until the last embers of the braziers faded. Then, in the great oblivion of sleep, Baghdad would cradle its dreams and chimeras, and the jugglers of words would fall asleep and, at the foot of the mud wall, Ahmed slept, like a bundle left by time in the heat of a summer's night, the same heat that kept the young of Baghdad from sleeping.

In the suqs of the round town, in the artisans' stalls and workshops, people were beginning to talk of this night-time storyteller, this old man who had once known legendary men of whom no trace remained. Ja'far's palace was abandoned: the Ksar al-Tin, the splendid residence of the Barmakids, belonged now to a prince's family who never came. The vast salons, the gardens, the silent and deserted patios had forgotten their past. And now, here was this old man, reopening the doors to the full sunlight, making the fountains dance and the rose bushes flower. You only had to come to the great square after nightfall for princes and servants to come back to life, for the basins to be lit up, and for the reflection of one man's face to hover amid the festivities, a shifting silhouette that silence would erase.

Throngs of people were now gathering around Ahmed, but did he even see them? Sometimes they found him already squatting there, murmuring confusedly between his teeth, or completely silent, closed in on himself, with his stick beside him; sometimes, helped by a child or alone – step after halting step – he would be the last to arrive. He would slump down without looking at any-one or, if his eyes did seem to look into the crowd, no expression could be distinguished there. And then, suddenly, as soon as this old man began to speak, as soon as he had found his past, his expression became full of life, his head and his hands no longer trembled, he was as if strengthened by the message he had to pass on, as if his memory, containing some powerful drug, filled him for a time with an exceptional strength and lucidity before then leaving him even more bent, even more wasted, even more destitute.

It was the sixth night and the wind rose, blowing up dust and swelling the abayas. Ahmed began to speak.

Baghdad, Baghdad, our town lay before us in the verdant countryside of that early spring. After four months, we came once more to the high clay walls, the dome of the palace, the golden horseman, that special light and smell, colours of earth and fire beneath the sinking sun. A flock of sheep was grazing at the foot of the walls and the young shepherd watched us arrive, shading his eyes with one hand. At the head, my master and I; behind us, the cavalry and the mehara riders. We were all silent. When we were right up by the first rampart, we stopped. A few horsemen were coming towards us: we recognised them; they were from the caliph's household. Harun was there, then; he had come back. Ja'far's hands were trembling, and I knew that he was prey to an extraordinary emotion; I drew near to him. A rider broke away from the small group and rode up to us.

'May peace be with you, Ja'far ben Yahya. We have heard of your victories in Syria. The caliph, our master, rejoices at them, and invites you to join him.'

Ja'far started. He was so pale that I thought he would fall from his horse. He managed to control himself, however, and, by some unimaginable effort, he spoke with a calm and detached voice:

'And may peace be with you, Selim ben Khaled. Would the caliph allow me to go to my palace so as to be worthy of appearing before him?'

'The caliph expects you immediately, Ja'far. Follow me. Your father and brother are with him.'

We rode through Baghdad surrounded by a multitude

of people who shouted with joy as we passed. The army was covered with glory, and, from the depths of the suqs, from obscure houses, everyone had come to this great celebration of our return. Was Ja'far thinking of how Harun had accompanied him to the ramparts on the day of departure? Or was he simply thinking that they were going to see each other again and that his own destiny would soon be decided?

We entered the great courtyard of the white marble palace. Ja'far looked about him. Nothing had changed. Everything was as it had been when he was honoured and powerful. We dismounted and walked through the first hall, the guard room, the inner gardens. The Council Chamber, our destination, was ahead of us; the door was open. The first person I saw in the half-light of the ebbing day was old Yahya, radiant and upright; then, Fadl, at his side, kindly and proud. Then, at last, I saw the caliph and, near him, Fadl al-Rabi. He was the first person my master saw. Standing in front of the painted door where blue birds perched on silver branches with gold leaves, Ja'far, pale, motionless, his hand on his heart, was staring at Harun, and Harun, looking straight ahead, in appearance perfectly calm, returned his stare. Everyone seemed frozen in the absolute silence. It was Fadl al-Rabi who spoke first:

'Come forward, Ja'far, the caliph desires to welcome you and congratulate you on your victories, the glory of which is already known to us.'

Ja'far started, and I thought he was going to throw himself on Fadl and kill him; but he controlled himself and stepped forward. Standing before the caliph, he made to kneel, but Harun took him by the shoulder.

'My brother is welcome in the caliph's house; may God be with him.'

Harun's voice was a little higher than usual and his

intonation was different. He was absent from the words he spoke.

'Tonight I am holding a banquet in your honour, Ja'far ben Yahya, and in the honour of the leaders of the Arab guard. I shall be happy to hear you tell of your successes. Go now and be with your kinsfolk; they are waiting for you.'

Without glancing back, he turned and went out, followed by the Syrian. Ja'far was transfixed, his expression utterly blank. One of his hands had tensed over the pommel of his dagger, the other was trembling at his side. His father came up and embraced him. At this, Ja'far seemed to come to life a little, and he smiled at his brother, who embraced him in his turn; but I knew that inside he was utterly dead.

Together, we made our way to Ja'far's palace, where a crowd of friends and servants were waiting for us. Precious perfumes were burning in his apartments. Rare fruits and flowers had been set out in bowls. Yahya and Fadl would not leave him. Everyone wanted to embrace and congratulate my master; in every place there was joy, save in eyes. He smiled, spoke, gave thanks, but I could tell that he wanted only solitude and silence. At last, they left him so that he could bathe and wash for the caliph's feast. He stretched out on his couch and I did not speak to him, for I knew he did not want to speak. I gave him a long massage. Slowly, he grew more relaxed; he turned to me.

'Ahmed, it seems to me that the Syrian has won.'

'No, master, Harun was not free in his presence. Only tonight will you be able to judge. If the caliph does not take you to his side for the meal, then your chances are slim. Beforehand, however, you must be hopeful; you must. Ja'far al-Barmaki will never give in to Fadl al-Rabi without a fight. The caliph still loves you. I can tell.'

Ja'far laughed. It was his first sincere laugh.

'Ahmed, Ahmed, you are like those holy men who see nothing but goodness everywhere. But you are not a wise man, you are a fool.'

'Perhaps, master, but I never lose my convictions.'

I dressed Ja'far magnificently for this meal, magnificently and simply. He wore a kaftan in white silk with a high collar and fastened by small buttons, an embroidered blue satin belt and a golden chain that the caliph had given him. On his feet, sandals of golden thread and, at his side, the dagger inlaid with sapphires that he had worn at that first banquet when Harun had chosen him. We saddled his horse in blue and gold and I dressed in blue. We set off with Yahya and Fadl, wrapped in woollen coats. To me, the journey there seemed infinitely long. It was cool and the heavens in their starry finery were dazzling. 'If I see the star of Venus,' I thought, 'my master will win.' I looked up and saw the star. And there, immediately, was the palace, rising up before us.

Unforgettable vision of warm smooth white marble lit by thousands of torches and lamps. The translucent, illuminated fountains seemed to be singing in this unreal twilight. On the inner patio, aviaries and glasshouses full of exotic flowers had been set out in front of the caliph's apartments where the feast was to be given. Lined with black and silver hangings, the great room was like a gigantic Beduin tent. On either side of the door, two hangings were tied back with silver braids to reveal the lighted copper chandelier, and a multitude of exquisitely coloured rugs were strewn across the floor. The tables were huge silver trays inlaid with vermeil and surrounded by cushions. A heavy perfume impregnated each curve, each fold, each hanging curtain. The guests were already seated, and were waiting for the guest of honour and the caliph. Sitting on the floor, their legs crossed, they instinctively struck the attitudes of their fathers; this sumptuous tent had been pitched in the Baghdad night just as those of their ancestors were for-ever pitched in the night of their memories.

Ja'far, with his father and Fadl, was led to the great table, slightly apart, where the caliph would sit. The two leaders of the Arab guard were already there and they greeted him. One of Harun's cousins and the brother of queen Zubaydah were also present. Putting his hand to his forehead, his mouth and his heart, Ja'far returned each greeting. They were now waiting for the caliph.

He came, and he was alone. Fadl al-Rabi was not at his side. Harun motioned his bowing friends to be seated, then, followed by his black slave, headed for my master's table. They were all standing there, waiting for the caliph to choose who would be at his side. Harun looked at his tutor and motioned him to his place, then looked around him, as if hesitating: when his eyes met my master's he grew pale and pointed to the cushion to his right.

'Be seated at the place of honour, beside your caliph, Ja'far ben Yahya; you have deserved it by your victories.'

Ja'far bowed. For the first time in many months they were side by side. Harun had changed. All his youth, all his joy in life seemed to have left him. He looked austere and pious and yet his mouth, his body, his voice and his hands still revealed in him a sensuality, a taste for life which were merely hidden beneath the surface. The necklace of beard and the fine moustache that surrounded his mouth made his face seem rounder, and almost juvenile, given the austere manner he had adopted. He was wearing a black abaya with gold brocade and a white kuffiya folded over his shoulders.

The food was brought in: whole roast sheep, herbs, vegetables, dishes of rice and semolina sprinkled with saffron and chopped mint. A young man was singing to

music from a cithara and a tambourine; like the light of
the torches and the perfume of musk and roses, his warm
carnal voice seemed to caress the silver and copper, the
silks and wools, the dark or pale skins, the black cords of
the kuffiyas, the satiny epidermis of lips, the dark soft
moustaches. The caliph beheld Ja'far; Ja'far's eyes were
shining brightly.

'I have important news for you, my brother. Your
success deserves a reward. I have nominated you governor of Khurasan: you shall be my representative there –
no one deserves my confidence more fully than yourself.
You shall leave as soon as possible.'

The light from an oil lamp placed on the ground
played over Ja'far's face, surrounding each of his features
with shadows and with a dancing light that made his
beauty strange, inaccessible. He put his hand on his
heart; his eyes were fixed on Harun's.

'Commander of the Believers, you are placing in me
a confidence of which I am unworthy, and I thank you
for it. I shall go to Khurasan as soon as you desire it.
Tomorrow, if you ask it of me.'

To the jangling beat of the tambourine, and the
weeping of the cithara, the singer was chanting words
of love and war, the sorrow of a departure. He was
gently rocking to and fro and had closed his eyes. The
smell of grilled mutton and of spices now mingled with
the perfumes. The caliph seemed unhappy.

Harun spoke again. 'I have been on a pilgrimage,
Ja'far. When I was praying to God, I realised that my
life had not always been as He wished.'

'Is it God's will that men should refuse happiness?'

'No, Ja'far, but that they should perhaps find a different
kind of happiness.'

Wine was served in cups of silver for the guests, and of
gold for the caliph. Harun drank and, as he drank, his

eyes were on Ja'far; everything within him was fighting against his need of my master, against an emotion he could barely control. As for Ja'far, he seemed calm, almost distant, and only I knew that he was like a man standing over an abyss, ready to fall. When he had heard the news of his departure for Khurasan, he had not reacted. Did it matter to him? Something else was at stake now, something more than mere staying or leaving.

The servants brought the sheep, quartered, with the eye on a golden plate. Harun took it. The corners of his mouth were trembling slightly. He was no longer sure of winning the battle he was fighting. The Syrian was absent and the presence of Ja'far at his side obliterated even the memory of Fadl al-Rabi. Then, supreme honour, the caliph opened his hand and offered the sheep's eye to Ja'far. My master took it, put his long fine fingers on Harun's and pressed them, and his eyes caressed the caliph with such sensual emotion that Harun suddenly seemed lost.

'Ja'far,' he murmured, 'Ja'far, why did you come back?'

'Since we parted, the only happiness I sought was that of seeing you again, and God is my witness that no other being can boast of having even brushed me with his hand during the time of our separation.'

A second singer had joined the first and, to the beat of the tambourines, the two voices came together to celebrate spring, the green of the countryside so bright that it borders on yellow, streams tinkling like silver, and young girls with skin the colour of honey and amber.

'Ja'far, how could I forget you? I have tried, I have prayed: I see now that I have failed. I want you to leave for Khurasan as soon as you can.'

'I shall leave, master, but I shall spend all tomorrow by your side.'

Around the table, the other guests were talking among

themselves in low voices, respecting the caliph and my master's conversation: they no doubt suspected that something important was happening. Fadl ben Yahya himself, so austere and so pure, was watching his brother with something akin to anxiety. The Barmakids knew that their destiny depended mainly on the caliph's love for Ja'far. Standing behind my master, I saw and heard it all, and each instant was like a ball thrown by a juggler – unstable, precarious, uncertain.

They exchanged a few words in such low voices that I could not understand them. Their arms touched, they were rubbing shoulders, and not even the servants were able to separate them when they tipped the silver ewer over the golden bowl to wash their hands. Harun drank, and each cup brought him still closer to my master. Their thighs were now touching and this contact so overwhelmed them that they could not look each other in the eyes. At this exact moment, I knew that Ja'far's love for Harun was real, that he was feigning nothing. His energy – so long straining towards Baghdad – his anxiety and his uncertainty, all were now exploding in a shower of violent emotions.

The lamps were smoking. To the airy sound of a flute, and with tambourines punctuating the end of each sentence, a third singer with a husky voice was singing the pleasures of love.

Northern wind, can you not see that I am crazed with
love and so visibly tired?
Give me the breath of Bathna's air and by your grace
breathe on Ja'mil too,
And say to her: Little Bathna, give me but a little part
of you, and then more than that little . . .

At last, in a deep but clear voice, Ja'far said: 'My lord, I am dying with love for you.'

The singers were clapping their hands and beating the ground with their feet. The heat in the vast tent had grown intense, and the odour of musk was intoxicating. The wine flowed clear and cool, and the musicians all together were singing:

My spirit embraced yours even before we were created
And even after we had become seeds ripening into life . . .

The torches projected their shadows on the black of the cloths, and their sheen was in itself brilliant like a sun in the silvery night of the vast tent, infinite space cast into this moment of our life – like a bridge between our dreams and eternity.

'Ja'far, each moment of my existence without you is like a death. I want so much to be myself, and yet my only desire is to melt into you.'

Now their eyes had met. Was it the noise of the tambourines and the flutes that stopped them speaking, or was it their desire for each other which tightened their throats and made them pale?

The sweetmeats arrived, pyramids of sugar, almonds and honey – gold and blond in the vermeil dishes, bowls of dates and rare fruit, curdled milk, compotes in cups of blue-tinted Chinese porcelain. Harun waved them away. He took Ja'far's hand and it seemed to me that everything had stopped, was suspended in time. I could only just hear the musicians, and the guests grew hazy under the white or black of the kuffiyas, shifting in the yellow lamplight in which only the silver sups of rosé wine could be distinguished. And, amid these hazy outlines, floating in an aureole of light, voices, silhouettes and odours, all I saw clearly was the caliph as he got up and left the room and was followed by Ja'far. The tent flaps fell back into place in their wake and the music drowned out the noise of their steps.

Ja'far did not return either that night or the following day. The caliph had left the palace; no one knew where he had gone. A return, and then a disappearance. Ja'far and Harun needed a different rhythm, longer hours spent out of the sun. I spent my day in the garden watching the growth of flowers I did not see. The following night brought my master back to me, and I saw by his pallor, by the lines around his eyes, and by his serene detachment, that that sunless and moonless day had given him the new warmth that glowed in his eyes. Because he had wanted him more than anything else, and because he had won him back alone, my master was now truly in love with the caliph. Balance of feelings, now light, now heavy; he who can refuse always has the last word. Ja'far had saved and then lost himself. The reins of his destiny were no longer in his own hands.

My master stretched out on his bed and closed his eyes.

'Tomorrow we leave for Khurasan,' he told me. 'Make yourself ready and leave me to sleep.'

At dawn, a few hours before our departure, while his friends and servants were preparing, Ja'far left his palace wrapped in a simple grey woollen coat and galloped to the caliph's residence. When he joined me, he was so overcome with emotion that he could not speak.

In the courtyard, horses and mules stood ready in the sullen and drab light of morning; we were cold and sleepy. It made our hearts bleed to leave Baghdad. Some of us already knew Khurasan, others were about to discover it. People said it was a wild and rough land, but it was our own, and Ja'far knew he would find there a population that wished him well. Upright, veiled and silent on her grey horse, the Afghan; behind her, a servant clutched a baby in her arms. She had not seen Ja'far since his return, she did not know if my master still wanted her, but still she came with their children. Ja'far rode past her; their eyes met, and that was all. We set off for Meshed, that faraway town where we would now live.

Interminable journey across rough and desolate country. The towns we stopped in were austere, dirty. We slept in big, freezing houses, often rolled up in our blankets and lying on thin rugs. The spring that was already caressing the terraces and gardens of Baghdad was no more than a distant hope in the east. One morning, in the Diyala valley, we awoke to find snow all around us, and the sight of the mountains, white in the sunlight, made us stop to marvel at such beauty. We had been on the march for ten days and there were many oases, clumps of trees like green patches on the red of the earth; the inhabitants, who were poor, offered us their fruit and milk. One night, in a villager's house, Ja'far and I were warming ourselves at a great brazier, side by side. We had stayed huddled in our coats, because of the cold; we were silent. I looked sadly at my master.

'You are thinking about the caliph, aren't you, you are wondering why he let you go?'

'I am wondering nothing, Ahmed. The caliph does as he pleases. He can keep himself away from me but he cannot take away my memories.'

'But will you be able to live on memories alone, my lord?'

'No, you are right, Ahmed, I am cold and I am bored: have them call for Amina.'

She came, dressed in a long black coat which she turned up over her face when she saw me. She had grown slimmer since our expedition to Syria and her eyes were enormous.

'Sit down,' said Ja'far, 'and warm yourself. Ahmed will make you some tea.'

94

I boiled some water. I could not bear to serve this woman, but I did not show it. I brought them glasses and, as I was about to retire, Ja'far motioned me to stay.

'She is yours if you want her, Ahmed, I give her to you for the night. Don't you want to taste a woman's body at last?'

Amina was silent. Her eyes were lowered but I could see her taut mouth and her hands as they tensed round her glass of tea. Why did Ja'far play these games with those who loved him? Was he trying to avenge his passion for the caliph? His handsome face had clouded over, he was smiling and his smile was almost painful.

'You know full well, master, that I love only you; the same is true of Amina. What you are asking is impossible.'

'You feel no desire for this woman, then? Well, I do desire her, so get out!'

His voice was dry and hard. I knew he was unhappy.

We had been on the road for fifteen days. We had passed Hamadan and were heading towards Qum, still following the valley, tired now of these snow-covered mountains, walls rising between us and the sun. Since that night with Amina, Ja'far had remained sombre and violent; his body was marching west, but his will, his heart, all that was best in him, had stayed behind in Baghdad. He was tired now of travelling, tired of his suffering and of the weight upon him of others' eyes. We hardly spoke to each other. I made his meals, sought blankets for him, lighted braziers, heated the tea. The governor of Khurasan was living like a pauper and suffering like an adolescent. At night, I watched him sleep: only then did his features relax. He slept little and ate less. His expression had become distant and his beard was growing, making him older; I did not dare implore him to take better care of himself.

We had been marching for nineteen days when we reached Qum, barely half the distance we had to travel. It was a large and prosperous trading town. Situated at a crossroads, it was a stopping place for caravans. They rested in the huge caravanserais at the city gates, just behind the ramparts. Persian, Pashto, Kurdish, Urdu and other more distant tongues, with their lilting or coarse intonations, all were spoken here. The faces around the fires were craggy, washed by the winds and the rains of the endless roads that led to the setting sun, to wealth, to towns woven from silk and gold.

The city gave us a warm welcome. Ja'far seemed to relax when he saw the house that had been put at his disposal; the wind did not blow there; hangings and rugs were everywhere. A meal had been set out and braziers burned in every room. After the austerity of the road, this house, a rich merchant's, seemed princely to us. Ja'far asked for a bath and I gave him a massage. For the first time since our departure, he seemed almost happy.

'We shall stay here for a few days,' he told me. 'I need to rest. Sometimes I feel as if there were somebody else living inside me.'

Outside, it was raining, an end-of-winter rain, fine and freezing. He dined by the fire while a musician played on the lyre. The wine in the cups was vermilion. In the perfume burners, jasmine and mandarin gave off their fragrances. I stood behind my master, serving him. At the end of the meal, he made me sit beside him.

'Ahmed,' he asked, 'when will we see Baghdad again?'

He did not wait for an answer, and I did not give one.

Ja'far went to bed early. He asked for Amina but, thinking better of it, decided to remain alone.

'They say there are beautiful women in Khurasan,' he said with a smile. 'I must learn to wait.'

'All Iranian women are beautiful, master.'

'Yes,' replied Ja'far, 'but what do you know about it?'

And, lying flat on his stomach on his bed, half-covered by a white wool blanket, he fell asleep. I stayed there for a long moment, watching him, then lay down on a rug at his feet and fell asleep in my turn.

It was still night when someone knocked violently on the door. I jumped to my feet. Ja'far sat up. I lit a lamp with the last embers of the fire and went to open up.

'Who is it?' I asked from behind the door.

'A message from the caliph for Ja'far ben Yahya.'

Ja'far was now on his feet.

'Open,' he ordered.

I opened the door. A man stood before us, soaked and exhausted. His hands were trembling. He had a letter, which he held out to me.

'Are you Ja'far ben Yahya?'

'I am he,' said my master and, stepping forward, he took the message.

The man took his leave. Where he had stood, a few brown drops of water grew round on the terracotta floor. Ja'far broke the caliph's seal and unrolled the letter. Few words were written there, but they were in Harun's own writing.

'Come back Ja'far,' the letter said, 'I cannot bear your absence. I am waiting for you.'

Ja'far let out a great shout – a wild, triumphant, mad cry; his eyes were shining like those of a wild animal but his laughter was that of a child.

'To Baghdad, to Baghdad, Ahmed, this instant!'

'Master, we must wait for day, pack our bags, see our hosts . . . '

'No Ahmed, you and I are leaving, this very moment. Go and saddle our horses and fetch our coats – that will do – there isn't a moment to lose. Go on, go on!'

He slipped on some woollen trousers, boots, a short shirt, a turban, a coat; I had already gone.

Ahmed revived, he straightened; the metamorphosis was abrupt, obvious. His eyes were shining and his face was suddenly alive, almost beautiful; his dirty, torn clothes now hung on him like the coat of a prince. Yes, in the space of a few brief instants, Ahmed recaptured the youth and enthusiasm of those long-forgotten days, the dust of the past that time had scattered into the four corners of his memory. For the first time, the old man looked at the crowd surrounding him and gave a chuckle like the creaking of a door to an abandoned residence, blown one stormy evening by the wind.

No, none of you, poor people of Baghdad, can imagine our return. Will I myself be able to tell it? May God come to my aid. But there are moments that no word can uncover. How can I describe our horses galloping through the valley amid the dazzling whiteness of the mountains, the foam thick at the corners of their mouths and their hindquarters steaming, and Ja'far leaning forward over his horse's neck, looking into the distance there, there to the west. We stopped for a few instants to let the horses breathe and to eat a handful of dates, a few dried fruit, then we rode on. The first night, we slept in a shepherd's tent, lying on the ground in our coats, eating only a few olives, a dry biscuit and some goat's cheese given by the shepherds. As men and beasts huddled together, I thought of the fabulous wealth of the Barmakids, of their palace, their libraries, their gardens, and I looked at Ja'far there among the poorest of men – indifferent, superbly happy. We went on our way at dawn, seen off by the entire camp. A young girl had made some tea. Her face was uncovered, as country women's are, and she could not take her eyes from my master's face. Because of these few moments of a life lived in poverty, this girl would remember for ever the image of a beauty beyond her imagining. Ja'far saw her staring and held out to her a gold coin. She refused. Her father, with a single, precise gesture, collected it and hid it under his robe with a thousand words of thanks and a thousand blessings. At dawn, alone by an orchard full of sleeping goats, we said our prayers.

A little way before Hamadan, Ja'far's superb stallion began to limp, and we slowed to a walking pace.

'I shall change him in the town,' said my master, 'we cannot wait.'

'Change your stallion, leave Rajja, master! Can you really mean it?'

'Nothing else matters to me now, Ahmed, but to arrive in Baghdad. My life is like an arrow in a taut bow; I need speed and wind, I need to take off for the sun on the horizon; it dazzles me, but that is where my destiny leads me. Ahmed, the caliph has asked for me and I am running to him; God knows that I am not going fast enough.'

In the town we looked for a horse. We were led to an innkeeper who had some poor thin exhausted-looking beasts. None of them would ever get us to Baghdad. Ja'far sat at the inn and sent me to deal with the matter. I had to act quickly. I led Rajja by the bridle and went to the residence of a merchant who, people had told us, possessed some fine horses. The merchant was out; the servants could do nothing. Someone went to fetch him from the suq. Time slipped by and I grew anxious at the thought of my master's anger. Rajja looked at me sadly. Perhaps he understood that we were going to abandon him. At last, a fat vulgar man arrived: he was wheezing.

We greeted each other.

'Who are you?' he asked.

'The servant of Ja'far ben Yahya al-Barmaki, governor of Khurasan; he needs a horse; his own mount is lame.'

The man took one look at me and burst out laughing.

'You, the servant of Ja'far al-Barmaki, the caliph's sweetheart? Where then is this picture of beauty on earth, this extraordinary man about whom all the merchants from Baghdad are always telling us? You mean to tell me, friend, that he is in our town? Our young men had better look out then, and our young girls will have to go into hiding!'

I stepped back.

'Merchant, for just one of the words you have spoken, my master would kill you. You do not know the power of the Barmakids. I have no choice but to leave you.'

And, taking Rajja by the bridle, I turned away. He stopped me.

'My friend, I was joking. The horse is superb. If your master wishes to exchange it, then let him come in person. I should like to see such a man. Leave the stallion here and go!'

I ran to the inn. Ja'far was waiting for me, beating his riding crop against his boot. I explained the merchant's request to him but did not mention what the man had said. Ja'far rose and followed me. We arrived at the merchant's house. He was waiting for us in the hall. The fat man bowed and gave us a servile greeting. My master answered him curtly.

'I am in a hurry, merchant, show me your horse.'

'Would you do me the honour of taking tea in my house?' asked the man, bowing and scraping.

'I told you I was in a hurry, my friend; give me your horse in exchange for my stallion. You will not lose out in the bargain.'

'What would you know of that, my lord? Baghdad is not the only wealthy city in the land.'

Ja'far was growing impatient.

'I have no time to waste, merchant; have your horse brought here.'

The fat man was now looking hard at him.

'Then you really are Ja'far al-Barmaki?'

Ja'far nodded.

'I am.'

'I have heard about you. You are famous for your beauty and for the love you inspire.'

Ja'far had tensed. He was pale.

'What do you mean by that, merchant?'

'You know, my lord, the Prince of the Faithful . . . '

Ja'far did not let him finish his sentence: drawing his dagger, he was upon him with one bound. I knew that he was capable of killing the man and I held him back in my arms.

'Master, leave this dog be. His death will only delay us further.'

Ja'far knew that I was right and stepped back. Then, taking his riding crop from his boot, he struck the merchant full in the face, twice.

'Never pronounce the caliph's name again. It is soiled in your foul mouth.'

And since the merchant, who had fallen to the ground, was protecting his face, and since none of his servants dared to intervene, Ja'far said:

'Go and fetch the horse from the stable, Ahmed.'

I ran off. A man showed me the way. I took the beast that looked the most handsome – a young mare – and returned, leading it by the bridle.

Ja'far was outside the house. He mounted the horse then, seeing Rajja tied up by the door, drew his dagger and, with a single stroke, cut the stallion's throat. When the beast was on the ground, he laid his hand on its head and looked at it lovingly.

'You are too noble an animal to belong to such hyenas, Rajja. May peace be with you, adieu.'

He jumped on to the mare and, cleaving through the crowd that had gathered outside the house, we galloped away. One of the fat man's servants came to close the gate of the residence and the children gathered around the horse and watched it die. I thought of Tarek and a lump came into my throat.

We galloped until nightfall, walking our horses only for a few brief instants. The temperature was becoming milder and near Kermanshah we saw the first fruit trees in blossom.

'At last,' said Ja'far, alighting for the evening prayer, 'at last solitude and silence. We shall sleep here.'

'Do you not want to go to the village, my lord, to ask for hospitality for the night?'

'No, Ahmed, I want to stay here. I could not bear to see other men today. Besides, we shall only stay here for a few hours. We shall leave before daybreak.'

I made the horses lie down and we stretched out beside them on our coats; we had eaten nothing, just drunk a little of the water from our gourds.

The moon was full, half hidden by light clouds like the veiled face of a woman. I waited for Ja'far to fall asleep and then fell asleep myself. I dreamt that the orange and cherry blossoms became stained with blood and that, drop by drop, it was dripping on to our faces, like a caress, or as if from a scratch: it was only the petals falling on us in the light night breeze.

Ja'far roused me before dawn. He was ready; he had washed his face and hands and said his prayers. His beard, which he had shaved at Qum, had started to grow again. He was lean, tired. Seeing him, the caliph would know how keenly he had desired to be with him. Behind my master's dirt and fatigue, he would see his endless, breakneck ride, his hope and his expectant joy. We stopped to eat and pray in a small town beside a river, a town of peasants and shepherds. They were nearly all absent at that time of day. The girls who were on their way to fetch water stared at us, laughing, the children ran around the horses and the dogs barked. We were poor travellers asking for hospitality, and it was granted us. We were served a vegetable stew with dry biscuits and hot tea. Before eating, Ja'far asked where the mosque was. He wanted to say his midday prayers. A child led us there. We pushed open a wooden door and entered a small room with an earthen floor and clay walls roughcast in white. A few poor rope mats lay on the floor, a lamp was burning. An old man was reading a parchment, chanting as he unrolled it. He did not even raise his head to look at us. Ring dance of flies in the narrow band of light that shone through a high window and spread into a fluid and variable pool on the black earth of the floor. The silence brought calm. Together, Ja'far and I laid our hands on our knees and began to pray. Before going out, I glanced at him and what I saw in my master's eyes at that moment – the gentleness, the serenity, the strength – made me believe in his happiness. His conviction joined with mine, his pleasure was my pleasure; had I ever known pleasure that was purely my own?

We ate. Ja'far gave another gold coin in payment and we set off on our unending ride. That night we slept in the camp of a caravan from the Punjab that was on its way to Baghdad. Around us, camels ruminated and squatting camel drivers cooked buckwheat cakes in the embers, dipping them in curdled milk. Ja'far ate with them. We slept side by side under a goatskin roof stretched between four wooden posts. The night was full of odours – camel dung, leather tannin and burnt wood. The moon was waning. The next day we would be in Baghdad.

In the morning, after drinking the boiling hot sugared tea, we went to greet the chiefs of the caravan. They too were going to Baghdad, but we would be there that night. Would these people ever suspect that the most powerful man in the round town, the man before whom all bowed and trembled, had eaten with them beneath the stars and slept at their sides? Would they even recognise him? Man is only a vague shape transformed by the hours and the days, now superb, now wretched, now immense and now minuscule. That is God's will.

We could recognise the countryside now: here Ja'far had stopped as a young boy to hunt, here we had walked as adolescents, here he had followed his father on horse-back when Yahya was still young. An oasis reminded us of our moist lips; its cool water had made us thirst for an even sweeter, more persistent moisture. On this stone wall, we had sat hand in hand, aroused even then by a touch which was the dawn of more violent emotions, more expert caresses; this village we had passed through at a great gallop, laughing as we chased chickens and goats; here Ja'far had fallen and I had kissed his bleeding knee. One by one, these memories flitted through my mind, each image recalling another and yet another, a whole past in which I curled up about myself. In those days, Ja'far was the future; all I had ever been was a memory.

Night was about to fall. We had eaten only a few dates and had drunk water from a fountain. Our goatskins were empty, we had to be in Baghdad before dusk, before the closing of the heavy gates that would open again only at dawn. One night of waiting, an unbridgeable gap of time that Ja'far refused even to consider. Quicker, still quicker, to arrive at sunset. Our horses were exhausted, and we ourselves barely recognisable: dirty, our clothes in tatters, our features drawn from the lack of sleep, the fatigue of the never-ending gallop, horsemen projected into the space of an eternal becoming, speeding towards what men call happiness; the fortified town with three ramparts, forever distant, forever out of reach.

The countryside around Baghdad was lush, the orchards were in blossom. The peasants were returning home on foot or on the back of their asses. The women, their headscarves over their faces, were hastening to return to their houses; the old men were talking in groups, sitting in the rays of the setting sun or leaning on their sticks, lives drifting on in the current of days.

Then, from the top of the minarets, one after another – powerful, imperative, raucous – the calls to evening prayer. Ja'far had never failed to respond to that call. He glanced at me; the gates would be closed in a few instants, just after prayer – and there, ahead of us, lay Baghdad . . . We drove our horses onwards; God would forgive us. We passed the first rampart, the second, the third. Night was falling, already the first gate was about to close; the guards standing on each side let through the last asses, the last traders pushing their carts, people on foot returning home. We pushed past them and they stood aside, thinking that only a powerful man could plough through the crowd like this with his riding crop, looking neither right or left. In front of the last gate we were stopped by a guard.

'Are you travellers?'

Ja'far kicked him aside with the tip of his boot:

'I am Ja'far al-Barmaki.'

The man bowed and we entered the town. Night had fallen. Behind the high rampart, surrounded by the towers where guards were constantly on watch, surveying each district, each thoroughfare, the crowds hurried through the streets. Behind the Khurasan gate, Baghdad, Baghdad and its alleys, its suqs, its palaces, its houses, its secret patios where roses and jasmine bloomed by the basins' sides. Ja'far stopped, breathed in the air and rubbed his face with his hands. He looked shattered.

Then, smiling at me, he said: 'We have done it, Ahmed, we have returned to Baghdad in four days!'

We were now before the palace. At the main gate, we were stopped by the caliph's guards but, recognising my master, they stood aside. We crossed the vast court-yard around the marble fountain; Ja'far dismounted and crossed the hall, where he was stared at in amazement, and then the guards' room. One of them stopped him. Ja'far pushed him away.

'Let me go, the caliph is waiting for me.'

The guard, who had drawn his sword, recognised my master's voice, put his hand on his heart and stepped back. Everyone was quiet, all eyes were on Ja'far.

We were on the patio, in front of the Council Chamber; to our right, the caliph's apartment. Ja'far was running now. I had difficulty in following him. Before the door of Harun's chamber, the black slave, erect, sword in hand.

'It's me, Muhammad,' said Ja'far softly, 'your master is expecting me.'

Then, silently, impassively, the slave stepped aside and opened the door. Thin, dirty, ragged, Ja'far entered the caliph's chamber. I stayed at the door. This was all I saw: Harun, who was conversing with a relative, suddenly rose and dismissed his guest. He was pale, transfixed, staring at Ja'far; then, he smiled, his eyes grew brilliant as if some new light had suddenly flared up in front of him. I saw Ja'far step forward and the caliph open his arms. Muhammad gently closed the door.

The wind was lifting the sand into long curving wreaths. A warm southern wind, dry and harsh. It chapped lips, made eyes water, minds anxious, bodies febrile and gestures impatient. A fine, impalpable sand was sweeping in under doors and through windows, depositing itself in the gardens, bowing the roses and making the blue tuberoses pale. The laurel flowers fell like the orchard fruits in the wind, still green, thrown away by children who laughed as they bit into them. Arabia was sending Baghdad its bitter perfume, its colours of pale mornings and golden evenings, its passion and its somnolence, its fleeting hopes and its eternal oblivion. At the gates of Baghdad, the infinite slowness was turning to transient activity; dogs howled at night and young women unable to sleep ran from one terrace to another shrouded in their veils. Bright-eyed boys caressed themselves, excited by the tautness of their bodies under their light robes; they sought the eyes of women, fugitive and laughing behind the mashrabiyahs. Old men dreamed – immobile, silent – and their life, fluid and shifting like the wind, drifted away under the gust of days that was wearing away the light dune of their existence, grain by grain.

Ahmed had been sitting in the great square for many hours now; he had closed his eyes and covered his mouth with a strip of his turban. He stayed there, one hand on each side of his thin body, his legs folded under him, now and then uttering words that were stifled by the grey cloth.

People were gathering round him but he did not move. The children nudged each other and laughed. Women chatted from behind the leather or the cotton masks that hid their faces. The men waited patiently.

The night was black, stifling. Blown by the wind, the light of a nearby fire caressed the edges of abayas and robes and imbued people's feet – bare or shod – with a glow like that of golden scarabs. Ahmed did not move.

The other storytellers had themselves abandoned their spells and power in deference to the magic that came from the lips of the old man. They were all there, and it was as if the great square of Baghdad was dancing in the wind around the silent Ahmed.

'Tell us about Ja'far, old man,' said a youth, 'we can do nothing without your memory!'

Then, at the name of his master, Ahmed opened his eyes and, without moving his head, looked around him; his gaze met that of the youth who had spoken; he contemplated him with a kind of interest, then looked down at the ground.

I am going to tell you about the days of Ja'far. Perhaps you have kept some weak gleamings of them in your memories, for they were dazzling like the sun at its zenith. My master had everything. Every day, the caliph would swell him with new honours as if he were a source and Ja'far a river. Ja'far was made commander of the caliph's guard, director of the post, of the mint and of the royal textiles. Engraved on golden coins, his name and effigy travelled to the very ends of the civilised world, united for ever with those of the caliph in the suqs, the countryside, the caravans and the ships – in the four corners of the Abbasid empire. His power was without limits, his powers beyond imagining.

One spring morning, Aziza gave birth to a son, Abd Allah Al-Mamun, and in accordance with the promise he had made, Harun came to take him in his arms and to entrust him to those of Ja'far, the boy's future tutor. Soon afterwards, the child would be acknowledged as second heir to his father, after prince Muhammad Al-Amin, Zubaydah's older son.

Aziza sometimes came to be with the caliph and Ja'far when they were together walking in the gardens, listening to music or reciting verse. Sometimes she even came to the Council where, concealed behind a curtain, she tried to understand how the two masters of Baghdad governed their empire. Her beauty had grown since her pregnancy. She was serene, and Harun loved her. At their first meeting, she wore a veil in front of Ja'far, but the caliph began to laugh.

'You belong to the same family, Aziza. Did you not know him when you were a child? You can let him see your face.'

And, from then on, she came without a veil. Did Ja'far remember her exquisite body in the glow of the oil lamp, upstairs in her father's house?

He never spoke of it, and Aziza did not seem troubled before him. She knew of Ja'far's relationship with Harun, and, in contrast to Zubaydah, who hated him, she loved him like a brother. Not for a second did she forget that she owed him her happiness.

Soon afterwards she was with child again and, sick with this new pregnancy, she had to remain in the women's apartments. This retreat, a minuscule event, was to be of capital importance for my master's destiny. The series of days leading Ja'far one by one to that January night had their source in this very moment, and no one could turn back the current. God knows where we are bound.

The caliph and my master began to miss the company of a lively, intelligent and gentle woman. Then Harun remembered a little sister, Abassa, an Arab princess, an amusing, cultivated and pretty child. She was only thirteen but the dawning of her womanhood was rich with the promise of many exceptional hours. She was invited, was charming, and stayed. Harun considered her with tenderness, Ja'far with respect and amusement. He was thirty. The child knew everything, understood everything, and spoke to wise men with candour and wit. She wrote verse, love poems which she read in the evening on the caliph's patio, beside the blue mosaic fountain. I was the only one to see her eyes as, fleetingly, hastily, they caressed my master. He treated her as a child; she was not yet veiled.

We left for Raqqa. Yahya and Fadl stayed in Baghdad, as did the princes of the caliph's house and the two heirs, al-Amin and al-Mamun. Fadl was not often allowed to see his pupil. Zubaydah tolerated him but had no love for him. She granted favours and friendship to the son of Al-Mansur's former chamberlain, to the Syrian Fadl al-Rabi; the caliph offered this man tokens of friendship in such profusion that surely they could not have much significance. Al-Rabi reigned over a powerful woman and over a small boy who would soon be powerful, and he knew that he was well placed. When he and Ja'far chanced to cross paths in the palace, they would greet each other but their eyes never met. Ja'far had the weakness to believe that this man had no power against him. Al-Rabi had the strength of his patience and his convictions.

Raqqa, on the banks of the Euphrates; Raqqa, surrounded by its horseshoe ramparts, open to the river, in the north of Syria; the aridity of its countryside away from the valley; the nearness of Byzantine territory, the enemy country that Harun wanted to bend to his will. An atmosphere both calm and tense. We were happy there, the protocol at court was simpler, and around us we had only our friends – young people, poets and men of letters, family friends, relatives. Of those the caliph and my master loved, only Abassa had stayed in Baghdad with her mother. Few women had made the journey from Syria: a few of Harun's concubines, whom he virtually ignored, and an impish little Sudanese girl who amused Ja'far.

In this arid environment, the palace garden took on a magical quality. The rarest flowers grew along marble walks, yew trees surrounded basins where gold and black fish swam; nestling together in large aviaries of wrought iron, the most fragile and colourful of birds, bright like insects or precious stones. We lived in this palace, cut off from everything, leaving it only to go hunting with our falcons. On these occasions, the caliph's bird was always the best. Ja'far no longer trained his hunters himself.

We were waiting for something, but no one, except the caliph and my master, knew what it was.

Then came the evenings of splendour when we understood why we were in Raqqa. First came the Byzantine ambassadors with their servants, bejewelled like princes. Harun did not receive them in person. It was my master who held a dinner in their honour. Dressed simply in black abayas, their heads covered by white kuffiyas with black cords, he and his friends received the Byzantines in their gold, their silk and their velvet. With their unaffected manner, Ja'far and his companions were of incomparable nobility. Such dignity and such loftiness made their dazzling guests look like parvenus. The feasting lasted three days. All that time, Ja'far remained impassive, distant, impenetrable, perfectly kind and yet totally indifferent to all. Then began the negotiations. The empress Irene wanted peace. She was ready to pay a tribute to the caliph and had sent Nicephorus Logothetes, her superintendent of finances, to parley. This was the future basileus whom Harun would see only to sign the treaty. The caliph had invested my master with the power to represent him.

The two men met alone. For a whole day, they shut themselves away in the Council Chamber with their scribes and – even though Nicephorus spoke Arabic reasonably well – their interpreters. Standing by the door, I saw Ja'far in profile, sitting in front of a low window that overlooked the gardens. His kuffiya hung down on each side of his face. He was quite still. The light entered at an angle and seemed to have sculpted his silhouette – his eyelashes, his straight nose, his mouth, his chin. He was sitting with his legs crossed and his hands resting on his knees – attentive, secret. Opposite, in the filtered light, bareheaded, dressed in a gold lamé robe with a belt, I saw Nicephorus, his mass of curly hair, his short nose, his fleshy mouth and powerful neck. Many years later, when Ja'far's head had been spiked on the bridge of Baghdad, and when, eight years afterwards, the skull of the basileus, who had been killed by the khan, was used as a drinking cup, I would reflect on the parallel destinies of these two men who, one spring morning, had sat face to face in that cedar-panelled chamber on the Syrian border. Handsome they both were, and both were sure of themselves. The passing wind, can you smell it? It is heavy with the exhalations of jasmine, it is sweet, it caresses your skin, makes you close your eyes and think of love, of youth; it brushes the leaves of the trees, then it becomes strong, violent, harsh, it parches lips, makes eyes water, closes doors and bends branches, snapping them with a dry, cracking noise. After that, it continues on its way. Can you see it in the distance? Everything grows calm; for you, it will have been merely a passing lover.

I have forgotten Raqqa. All I can see there are skulls, unable either to see or talk to each other. And, falling on their bleached bones, my tears seem to be escaping from their empty orbits to fall on the red silk cushions of the Council Chamber and spread like bloodstains.

Nicephorus and Ja'far reached an agreement. The caliph ratified it. Every year, the empress would pay a tribute, and Harun would no longer cross her frontiers. Mutual hypocrisy, false friendship; during the departure celebrations, Greeks and Arabs drank together, ate together, possessed the same women and then separated, never to meet again.

We spent the summer in Raqqa and, when autumn came, Harun desired to make the pilgrimage to Mecca. We returned to Baghdad. In the palace of the Barmakids, Fadl was waiting for his brother. This incorruptible, tolerant and philosophical man was about to lose himself and to shake the powerful edifice of his family. No one had foreseen it, how could they have done? Have not the very ramparts of Baghdad given way to the desert wind? I once knew them high, intact and impenetrable, and now I see the breaches grow bigger and the crows nesting there in winter. Fadl and Ja'far spoke at great length. In the evening, Ja'far informed me of his brother's desire to intervene in favour of Yahya ben Abd Allah and obtain permission for him to leave Medina. He also wanted to intercede on behalf of the Alids in Persia, to give them hope and liberty. Ja'far grew pensive. He knew of Harun's hostility towards the Alids but, in the depths of his conscience, he was on his brother's side.

As the days passed, by dint of listening, of watching and keeping silent, I had come to know Harun – his sensitivity, his intelligence, but also his pride, his susceptibility, his religious intransigence, his violence.

'Master,' I said, 'the caliph loves you. You are strong,

but do not weary his love, for if he withdraws it, then may God help you, nothing will hold you. Harun must be the unique object of your life. Yahya ben Abd Allah does not count.'

Ja'far laughed.

'Ahmed, what do you mean with all these moral values, these aspirations of the spirit? We, the Barmakids, owe it to ourselves to support our friends. What does the rest matter? I shall keep myself from getting involved in this request. Fadl is Harun's foster brother: the caliph cannot ignore that fact. I shall be absent from Baghdad the day my brother sees him. Are you satisfied, Ahmed?'

I looked straight at Ja'far.

'The caliph too will be satisfied, master, and you will rejoice to see him again soon.'

We left the same day on a hunting expedition which was to last three days. Ja'far enjoyed himself, galloping into the wind; he was not worried. When we returned, Yahya was standing there waiting for us, overcome with emotion, in my master's own chamber. Ja'far froze: he was still in his hunting gear and a smile hung about his lips.

'The caliph flew into a rage when he heard your brother, Ja'far. He has refused ever to see him again. Fadl has lost all his responsibilities at court, except as tutor to prince Al-Amin, may God preserve him. You must go and see Harun, my son, make him bend; my own intercession was of no use.'

Ja'far stood a few steps from Yahya: he had gone pale.

'Father, what are you saying?'

'Harun will no longer see Fadl, never again. You must make him change his mind.'

Then Ja'far understood; within a few seconds, his resolve was set.

'Father, I can do nothing for Fadl without bringing

about my own undoing. Let us leave time and forgetting to bring forgiveness and let my brother's name never be pronounced in front of the caliph, either by your lips or by mine. Persuade him to leave, to go away for a while; I shall not speak to him but my heart shall be with him. Tell him that. As for me, I shall stay with the caliph, for nothing can separate me from him. Nothing, nobody.'

Yahya considered his son for a long moment and bowed his head. Then, without saying another word, he went out. He suddenly seemed very old.

Not once did Harun and Ja'far mention Fadl. My master was charming, seductive. They laughed, drank, played at dice late into the night. Then he would follow the caliph to his chamber and the door would close behind them.

The next day, when Harun and Ja'far were eating together, my master asked:

'Isn't princess Abassa supposed to be coming back from Mecca soon?'

He had never spoken of Harun's sister before, but I knew that he sometimes thought of her. The caliph smiled, and his smile was ambiguous.

'She will be here soon, but don't you know that she is a woman now? You will no longer be able to see her as before. She will have to wear a veil in front of you.'

Ja'far was deep in thought. Abassa, hidden behind a mask or veil? Would he never see her face again then? Her wide black eyes, her fine nose, her ripe mouth, her small teeth, and – like a pink flamingo's – her neck? He himself was astonished at his disappointment. This little fourteen-year-old princess, proud of her Arab blood, amusing – yet so full of herself – what importance could she have for him? He would listen to her laugh and sing, play the lyre, recite poems, and it was well thus. The leather mask or the veil were nothing.

Aziza gave birth to a second son, Al-Mutasim, the future caliph. There were great celebrations in the palace and, on the last day, all the gardens were illuminated and there was a poetry contest. Behind each copse, each column, each fountain, in the rose garden and among the orange trees, in their simple white attire, musicians, jugglers, magicians and poets re-created the world, rolled it out in a serpent of fire and honey, of gold and of space, then wound it about the caliph's wrist. Harun, in the Bengal lights, looked like some jinni, and Ja'far at his side, like one of those ancient statues of unchanging beauty that exist in and for themselves until the end of time. Between two lines of musicians, Harun walked Ja'far to the end of the marble alley that led to the blue and green ceramic basin. To what? To a fragile form seated on the edge of the basin, wrapped in a transparent black coat spangled with pieces of silver: Abassa. She was masked, a light tulle mask through which her face could be descried. She was laughing.

'Do you recognise me, Ja'far?'

'Princess Abassa, I have not been able to forget you. Since your departure, you have never ceased to occupy my thoughts and my heart.'

He had adopted a light and playful tone, but I knew that he was almost telling the truth.

Harun looked at them both. Again, his face was wearing that ambiguous smile which frightened me. Then, he put his hand on Ja'far's arm and, without taking his eyes off his sister, said:

'And you, little sister, had you forgotten my friend's beauty?'

Abassa lowered her eyes then, quickly raising her head, she let out a little laugh.

'Ja'far's beauty cannot be forgotten, is that not so, my brother?'

Then the caliph slipped his hand into my master's and caressed it for a few instants – he wanted Abassa to see this – then let go.

'Will you walk?'

A group of musicians stood shaking tambourines and, between them, a dancer seemed to be stretching towards the sky: her feet were flying, her arms beat the warm air, her hips and belly rubbed themselves against the night. The musicians were swaying in rhythm. A little further on, in the bluish gleam of a Bengal light, an old singer was celebrating in a monotonous voice the epic ride of the horsemen of Islam to the edges of the world; the name of God, which he repeated continually, made his two young accompanists bow.

'Come and drink,' said Harun, 'I am thirsty.'

The three of them sat down under a copse of oleanders. There were cushions there, as there were all about the gardens. The May night was studded with stars; the air smelt of musk, sandalwood, wine, and of the desert. Everywhere, the music pounded time with tambourines and flutes, making it lose all notion of the passing hours, as if the world were grinding to a halt above Baghdad, fascinated by the celebration and by the dancing light of thousands of lamps. The Bengal lights made the water in the basin seem red and the blossom on the trees blue; they imbued nature with a strange, poetic, maleficent appearance. When I bent over the water I was frightened to see blood on our faces.

'Some wine, Ahmed,' Ja'far ordered.

I went to fetch a silver carafe of Cyprus wine and some goblets. I served them. Abassa raised her mask slightly to drink. Ja'far was watching her.

'Little sister,' murmured the caliph, taking the princess's hand, 'you know that, from now on, you must under no pretext unveil yourself before my friend.

That would be to give offence to God and to offend me, too, irremediably.'

Abassa bowed her head and did not reply. The caliph was still holding her hand.

'Do you love my friend, Abassa?'

'Whom you love, I love, my lord, and I am very attached to Ja'far.'

'You are right to be, and, on this very day when we are celebrating the birth of my son, who is in some way his own son too, I am going to prove to him the love that I bear him, a love that will never fail. Behold' – and he showed his left hand – 'look at the caliph's seal, sign of his absolute temporal power. Whoever wears this is the master of our world, he is feared to the ends of the earth and none can claim to be greater than he. This seal, I give it to you, Ja'far, for you are worthy to wear it, you are the dearest part of my heart.'

Harun took my master's hand and slipped the seal ring on to his finger. Abassa watched them, dumb-founded, then, for one long moment, she stared at Ja'far, serious now; then she understood his power, his influence, the fascination that he exercised on those around him, and I knew that at that moment she too was under his power, that she saw him as the most beautiful, the greatest, the most powerful of all men and that in her heart and in her child's body she desired him as one desires a mythical being – a being im-possible, untouchable, for to be possessed he had to be taken from the caliph. She spilt some of the wine in her glass and rose.

'My brother, I must leave, I must not tarry in the gardens with you. My mother and my aunts are waiting for me in the palace. We shall meet again soon.'

She folded the tulle over her face, covering it completely. But I could see her eyes fixed on my master's, and my master's on hers. Harun considered them both and, in the glow of the Bengal light, their three faces were coloured vermilion.

Abassa walked away. My master made to take the seal ring off his finger.

'Leave it,' said the caliph, 'I was not play acting, I am giving you my earthly power. Now you are my equal; we are as one.'

Ja'far knelt down, took the caliph's hand and kissed it. Harun, inexplicably, seemed almost unhappy, as if he had prescience of something terrible, or, perhaps, as if he even wished it. Softly, he said:

'Ja'far, I have given you everything you desired. From now on, there is nothing more you can ask of me.' And, in a firm voice, he repeated: 'Nothing more.'

I knew that he was referring to Abassa.

Hand in hand, they returned to the palace.

Later, Ja'far persuaded the caliph to give his seal ring to Yahya, his spiritual father. Since he wanted to honour their family so magnificently, then only the head of that family was worthy of such an honour and would know how to use it for the good of all. For his part, he sought only his friendship, nothing more, and he knew that he had it.

Harun's action did not increase the power of the Barmakids, for they already governed the empire, but it did enhance their prestige even further and it now seemed as if no wind could make them bend.

At the end of the summer, Harun desired to return to Raqqa and make his capital there. He had never missed a single pilgrimage or holy war, and had discharged both duties every year. Up there, in Syria, he would be nearer the field of battle, where God wanted him to be. The caliph's piety was great; he sometimes saw himself as God's terrestrial arm, and he hoped that the scrupulous performance of his duty as a Muslim would win him pardon for his weakness as a man. Yahya governed in Baghdad; the empire was in good hands, such powerful hands indeed that their grip sometimes oppressed the caliph. In Raqqa, he felt freer, greater. Ja'far followed him, along with Aziza and Abassa, the crown princes and all his loved ones. Queen Zubaydah also came and, with her, Fadl al-Rabi. Living side by side almost every day, Harun and the Syrian once more grew accustomed to each other. While never making him appear before Ja'far, the caliph summoned Fadl al-Rabi often.

The autumn was stifling in the Syrian desert. Harun and my master spent the evenings on the terrace listening to music or playing at dice. Abassa often joined them. She remained veiled and managed not to give any sign of her attraction to my master. These were happy, peaceful days; the caliph's eyes no longer had that strange glow that they had had before when he was in the presence of his sister and his friend. They laughed and it seemed that their understanding would never end. My master was thirty-two, Abassa fifteen. It was the year 185[801AD]. I remember it now as a door, a door at the bottom of a garden of delights, leading God alone knows where, and that no one wishes to open. Suddenly, a breeze starts up: at first, a gentle zephyr, then an increasingly violent wind; the door begins to creak, to shake, the hinges turn as if of their own accord: it opens, slowly, pushed by no human hand. Then as if drawn by some magic force, the garden of Eden disintegrates, hurtles through the open door and is seized by the void, the black, freezing desert, which swallows it up. Between the clay walls, the eyes see only desolation and emptiness, an arid, ravaged earth, as if ploughed by torrents of tears . . . Suddenly, the silence is shattered by the cawing of a crow: he is holding something in his beak, a shred of flesh. Where did he pick it up? No one knows; perhaps on the bridge of Baghdad . . . In the place of the unhinged door, a woman's face, a child's almost, with a calm, absent expression, is turned forever inwards, towards a ruined garden of Eden . . .

Ja'far hunted often and for many hours at a stretch, leaving at dawn and returning at night. It was as if he were trying to exhaust a body that refused to obey him, to break it, to master it. One morning, when, with myself and several falconers, he was preparing to set off, one of the caliph's servants came to inform him that Harun and Abassa wished to accompany us. Ja'far shouted with joy and, when the caliph joined him, kissed his hand.

'My lord, you could not give me greater pleasure and pride than by according me your company. God is my witness that I rejoice at it.'

The caliph looked at him, smiling. He had put his hand on that of my master, who was bowing to him.

'Do you not rejoice equally at the presence of my sister?'

'Less than at yours, my lord, but princess Abassa does me a great honour in following my hunt.'

She was standing behind the caliph, frail and minuscule in her riding outfit, her ample breeches, her embroidered boots, her tunic tightened at the waist and the short veil hugging her head, hiding the lower part of her face, leaving visible only her eyes, like those of a happy gazelle.

'Let us set off,' said the caliph, 'it will be a hot day. We must leave early.'

The dry earth flew up under the hooves of our horses. Abassa was a fine horsewoman, her small white mare flew like the wind and its mane and the edges of the princess's veil were like wavelets softly beating the blue of the sky. Harun and Ja'far followed her, side by side. Harun watched his sister, my master the neck of her horse. There was a feeling of unease between them, and its cause was there, galloping ahead of us, laughing. We stopped at an oasis to drink. The princess drew aside to lower her veil. She was hot, drops of sweat were running down her forehead and from her temples, and spattering the veil like tears. Then we remounted our horses and the three of them rode ahead of us at a walk.

The hunt was abundant. The princess's falcon killed a young gazelle, a bustard and a stray wild goose. She herself aroused the bird with her voice, and from her throat rose joyous and aggressive noises like those made by women when their men leave for war. Harun was tired. He stopped his horse under a clump of date trees near a well and desired to rest. Ja'far and Abassa went off so that their birds could take to the air for one last time. The caliph watched them fade into the distance, following them with his eyes as long as he was able. Finally he took some water in the hollow of his hands and poured it over his face.

There were four of us: Ja'far, Abassa, the princess's falconer and myself. Four people in a dusty valley, behind a hill that our horses had climbed at walking pace, panting. My master and the princess walked ahead. We were all silent. It was hot. The site was majestic and wild. We felt both oppressed and free at the same time.

We were watching, on the lookout for new game. The horses scratched the ground with their hooves and snorted. The heat seemed to dance on the ground like translucent smoke, drowning the herbs and the thorny plants in its ethereal fluidity. The falcons were growing agitated on their perches. Suddenly, clear and sharp in the silence, the cry of the princess's falconer rang out.

'There, there, a young fox!'

A small red shape, barely distinguishable from the

ochre of the earth, emerged from behind a quitch bush: it was running straight out into the open ground.

Simultaneously, Ja'far and the falconer unhooded their birds. The predators blinked and beat their wings; their clasps clicked. My master's falcon was the first to take flight and was immediately followed by Abassa's.

'Go, go!' cried the young girl.

The birds rose in the sky: slow, majestic, their wings spread, hovering in the breeze, rising and descending with the currents of the wind, both of them beautiful, impassive, cruel. Sensing danger, the fox froze, pricking up his ears; then, too late, he darted off; the falcons had seen him. Together, exactly together, they fell on the beast, each of them astonished at the presence of the other. The animal struggled, torn apart by beaks that sought to wound, to tear flesh. Then the two falcons looked at each other, and each tried to win the prey for itself alone, pushing the other aside with its beak and claws. The combat would only end when one of them was dead. The fox, taking advantage of this respite, fought free, but the birds fell on him anew, united for one instant before returning to their combat. The princess was wringing her hands.

'Go and separate them,' she urged the falconer, 'or they will kill each other.'

The man galloped off.

The three of us were together. I was behind them; Ja'far and Abassa were side by side in front of me. It was she who edged her mare closer to my master's horse, she who caused the flanks of the two beasts to touch and her leg to press lightly against Ja'far's.

He turned his head slowly and looked at her. Standing close to the birds, the falconer was snatching them from their prey; its gaping belly was bleeding profusely.

Abassa, too, turned her eyes towards Ja'far. Their

gazes met . . . was it a long meeting? Perhaps not, but I believe that the sun in the sky had stopped to look at them. Their destiny was waiting for them there, in that lost valley on the edges of the Syrian frontier. God is my witness that my master did not move. It was the princess who, looking straight into Ja'far's eyes, lowered the veil covering her face. It was a simple gesture of extreme audacity, an irresistible appeal that made Ja'far tremble with desire. She smiled and he smiled also. Her small hand sought my master's and slipped into it.

'Ja'far,' she murmured.

That was all, but it was enough for my master to know that the princess was offering herself to him. When would he take her? Neither of them knew, but both desired it more than their dreams, more than their futures, more than life.

The falconer was riding back with the fox slung across his horse and the two birds on his fist. With a quick movement, Abassa covered her face and, spurring her mare, rode away from Ja'far.

My master was pale. He closed his eyes.

'Let us return to the caliph,' he said.

They turned around. The princess and Ja'far avoided looking at each other and if by chance their eyes did meet, they became troubled as if blinded by the sun. Harun, on horseback, was coming to meet us.

AHMED'S EIGHTH NIGHT

The wind had been gaining in strength all day; the long gusts, burning and dry, made the inhabitants of Baghdad shut themselves up in their homes, slamming doors and windows, gathering in inner courtyards or in the penumbra of their houses. The terraces were empty, the streets and squares deserted. At the end of the afternoon, in the coolness of the suqs, a few shops opened, but customers were rare, and beggars taking shelter in the doorways of the mosques dozed, waiting for nightfall. When evening came, the great square was empty. It was hot. Who, then, would make their way through this torrid heat to breathe life into the night? What strange forms might dreams take in this tenebrious oven, in the humidity of the air and of the bodies that burnt with a desire that was forever renewed, forever without a home? Were the shades of Ja'far and Abassa there, embracing in this their beloved Baghdad? Who remembered them, except for this solitary old man who opened his arms to the wind to embrace his past? Tonight he was going to speak alone, or almost, and it was well thus, for the moments of love that he was about to revive would instantly disappear on the wind, to be blown to their resting place, perhaps nowhere, perhaps in the memory of the world.

My master loved Abassa as he had never loved any woman, because she was young, extremely beautiful and very learned, because, as the caliph's sister, she was an Arab princess of an exceptional lineage, and because he was forbidden to touch her, or even to see her face. His imagination, his taste for the impossible, his sensuality, all the elements needed to draw him towards Abassa had come together. She filled his thoughts and dreams, and in his embraces with Harun, or with other women, she was the one he possessed.

Abassa, for her part, avoided him; in his presence, she was sad and taciturn. Harun watched them, and that equivocal smile had now returned. He never left them alone and when he took his leave he demanded that his sister go with him.

Strange absence of a jaded, weary man, strange evenings when all three laughed together, with sorrow in their eyes. The caliph loved to caress Ja'far in front of the princess and to caress his sister in front of Ja'far. He took pleasure in their inner turmoil and their impotence. My master's passion for Harun gained new strength, as if he were pursuing him relentlessly, trying to destroy him – to annihilate him and to free himself. One night when I was standing behind the curtain of the caliph's bedroom, ready to leave, I saw my master caressing Harun's neck, his hair; his long fingers ran though the brown curls, over the cheeks, along the short beard, and on to the shoulders. Then the caliph turned to him with a smile.

'Would you like to possess my sister, Ja'far?'

My master froze.

'Why do you ask me that? Has some look or gesture of mine made you think such a thing?'

Harun began to laugh – tight-lipped, mocking, malicious laughter.

'Everything in you desires her, Ja'far – your body, your mind, your ambition . . . but you shall never have her, never. Forget her.'

And, leaning towards my master, he took his two hands and kissed them.

Sometimes he would speak to Abassa.

'See how handsome Ja'far is, little sister, look at his face, his perfect body. He is ardent, intelligent and valiant. You will never be able to find another man of his worth. But he is not for you. You shall marry an Arab prince: he will choose you soon.'

One day he added: 'I was thinking of Fadl al-Rabi; wouldn't he make a suitable husband?'

Abassa never seemed troubled. The strength and courage of this young girl were extraordinary.

'Fadl al-Rabi is not a prince, my brother, he is the son of a chamberlain.'

'Ja'far is the son of my vizier, Abassa, what is the difference?'

'But I shall not marry Ja'far, brother of mine, unless of course you desire it, for I shall obey you in all things.'

The princess was strong, certainly, but she had stopped riding and going out now and had lost her appetite. The caliph took his meals with her only when my master was absent, for he still did not permit her to raise her veil; they remained silent together. Without Ja'far, the caliph's pleasure was blighted.

Late one night, after a game of dice, quietly, as if speaking of some trivial subject, the caliph said:

'Princess Abassa is going to marry Fadl al-Rabi. I am rewarding this outstanding servant with my most precious possession.'

Ja'far went terribly pale and shuddered with nervous tension; the dice rolled on to the floor. At last, he turned to the caliph and, in contrast to his extreme tension, his expression was caressing and tender.

'My lord, don't do that, I beg of you.'

'And why not Ja'far? Fadl is a good servant and a friend!'

'He is a bore and already has two wives. Do you want

such a husband for little Abassa? Marry her off to any Arab prince and I shall be happy, but not to Fadl al-Rabi, not to him.'

The caliph lowered his head.

'We shall see about that. Besides, Abassa is still young, but I see that she is sad and I think she wishes to marry.'

'Speak to Aziza, my lord, she will find someone suitable for the princess. She is a woman of great wisdom and goodness.'

Harun did talk with the Persian woman and his attitude towards Ja'far changed. He no longer took pleasure in taunting him; he even looked on him with tenderness. There was a truce but, far from taking advantage of it, my master and Abassa avoided each other even more, for their mutual presence inevitably made them suffer.

Finally, one marvellous autumn morning in the rose garden, the caliph, Ja'far and Abassa were walking in the tender yellow light among the flowers; these were shedding their petals. Harun sat down on the edge of the fountain, took Abassa by the hand and made her sit by his side.

'Little sister,' he said slowly – and there was a brilliant light in his eyes – 'you are going to get married, for you are beautiful and you cannot remain alone.'

Abassa was utterly still. Her lowered eyes contemplated the flowers and the birds in the blue mosaic: they all seemed to be listening to her brother. The caliph continued, and his words fell between the murmurings of the water and the exhalations of the roses.

'Last night I spoke to princess Aziza. She made a request and I consented to it, but on one condition, which I shall tell you about presently. But, first of all, do you want to know the name of your future husband?'

Abassa was still silent. Ja'far stood before them,

plucking the petals from a rose, his hands tearing them off as if he wanted to make them share his own suffering. Harun had stopped speaking and was relishing their silence. Finally, he dipped his fingers into the basin, took some water in the hollow of his hand and, opening it, suddenly splashed it on the mosaic, wetting a faience golestan, the mythical bird of Persia, which was depicted there and was now shining splendidly in the sunlight.

'You are going to marry the being I love most in all the world, who is dearer to me than my own eyes – my friend, my brother, Ja'far al-Barmaki.'

Abassa could not prevent herself from giving a start. My master, tearing the last petals, threw away the stem and stared at the caliph. He did not dare express the slightest emotion; he was convinced that Harun was still joking. The caliph began to laugh.

'This prospect does not seem to bring you the joy it brings me, and yet it is pure wisdom to heed the words of princess Aziza. You see each other every day and my little sister is forced to wear a veil which gets in her way. Henceforth, she will be free in your company, Ja'far, and the three of us will be able to see each other without any constraints. She will be able to eat and drink with us and we shall be happy. Won't you be happy, my brother?'

'My lord, I shall do what you tell me to do. If it is your will that I marry princess Abassa, then I shall marry her; but you spoke of a condition.'

Abassa's eyes were shining as she watched Ja'far from behind her pleated veil of black cloth; she had sat up and her two hands were holding the side of the fountain; she was anxious, attentive.

'Yes, Ja'far, I spoke of a condition. You shall marry Abassa because it will be easier for our life together that you marry her, but you shall never consummate this marriage, never. You shall not touch my sister, you shall never be alone with her and you shall offend me beyond recall if you disobey. That is my will, do you accept it?'

Ja'far made a tremendous effort to control himself, not to throw himself on Harun and knock him down. The wrong that the caliph was doing him by giving him a woman that he could not touch was grave, and he was sorely tempted to show his disappointment and anger by reviling Harun.

'You are the master, my lord, I shall do what you demand, but first ask the princess if she consents to this marriage. I will not marry her if she does not wish it.'

Then Abassa stood up, straight and proud, and gave her brother a long, intense look; her eyes were both hard and full of pity.

'My brother, you are asking of me what no man has the right to ask of a woman, and if our father were alive now he would demand satisfaction of you for this. But you are the caliph, the master, therefore I shall obey you. I shall marry Ja'far and I shall stay away from him. However, he is still the man I love and you can do nothing to change my feelings. When will you wed us?'

'At the end of the winter, in Baghdad. You shall choose the moment yourself, and you shall decide on the celebrations I shall hold on your behalf, for you are the mistress of my heart and your desires are sacred to me.'

The princess was silent for a moment. Her anger seemed to have passed. She was pensive.

'Harun, you know how dear you are to me, and I know that you love me too. Ja'far is your brother, your friend; be careful; do not estrange those who love you, for solitude is the death of man. Alone, he is nothing. Do not forget it.'

And she made off down the alley, a fragile and light

silhouette in her long black gold-embroidered dress. Harun followed her with his eyes and then turned to my master.

'Ja'far, you will have to love me very much in return for the gift I have just made you; very much, and for a long time. Come with me, we are going to walk a little. I love this rose garden when the flowers are dying. It is like a silky, perfumed cemetery; each petal is the tomb of a few fleeting instants of summer and happiness. Let us not be like them, let us remain happy as long as we live; we must. Come, my handsome Ja'far, recite a poem to me to make me believe in happiness, to make me love you even more, and don't be upset, women are of no importance: they fade, they are as fragile as roses – the wind of our old age will sweep them away and we will remain, you and I, alone for ever.'

They were walking. Ja'far stopped, his face turned to the sun, his eyes closed. He spoke a poem which Harun listened to without once taking his eyes from him; he was contemplating my master's face with the expression of a desire so intense that it frightened me.

I should so like to know who she was
And how the night had come.
What was she, the face of the sun or the moon?
Was she an impulse of intelligence, given away by
its very activity
Or a vision of the mind revealed in me by thought?
Or an image formed in my soul by my own hope, that
my sight believed it saw?
Or, then again, perhaps she was none of these things
But rather some secondary sign sent by destiny to provoke
my death?

❧

My master asked to return to Baghdad. He wanted to see his relatives, take charge of his affairs and prepare his marriage. Harun granted this wish. They suffered to leave each other but this suffering was a trifle compared to the moral pain that was now their daily life. Abassa had said she was ill. Neither one of them had seen her again.

Ja'far took his leave of Aziza. He was already in his travelling clothes and a servant was holding his saddled horse in the courtyard. The princess received him in her ceremonial chamber, veiled, surrounded by her women and her slaves. They spoke of Baghdad, of things without importance – for other ears were listening. Then, as Ja'far was about to leave, she leant towards him.

'I obtained your marriage from Harun before he had imposed his condition. Refuse to marry Abassa, for the caliph is jealous of you. He loves you both. Beware.'

And, as a servant was approaching with a tray of dates and pastries, she spoke aloud:

'May your journey be blessed by good, Ja'far al-Barmaki, and may the peace of God be with you.'

Ja'far bowed and stepped back.

'And may the peace of God be with you also, princess Aziza.'

Then, looking straight at her, he added:

'We shall see each other again in Baghdad, at my wedding feast.'

Aziza knew then that nothing would stop my master from running to meet his destiny.

Ja'far left the palace, mounted his horse and galloped off as if he wanted to flee from Raqqa for ever. He would never see the town again.

In Baghdad, everyone was dazzled by the announcement of Ja'far's marriage. Were the Barmakids then going to climb so high? To unite their blood with that of the Prophet's family? They really were invincible, irresistible. Persians and Alids were merry; their hopes knew no limits. Everyone rushed to Ja'far's palace, everyone wanted to be his friend. Ja'far remained impassive, lofty, and this detachment was attributed to his justifiable pride: the blood of the Prophet and that of the Barmakids, mixed for all eternity! They were powerful, they were rich, and now they were entering into an alliance with the Arab family that guarded its purity more jealously than any other. Truly, God's eye was upon them!

Gold flowed like a watercourse in thaw at the end of winter. For his fiancée, Ja'far bought jewels, perfumes and the most beautiful dresses that human skill could weave. He wanted her to have everything, this young girl he would never touch, and when he thought of her in her finery, perfumed, covered with jewels, his body began to tremble. Then he had one of his concubines come to him – sometimes Amina, sometimes others – and he would stay with them until dawn without saying a word. In the morning he fell asleep; his face was drawn and sad.

Winter was over. The orange and lemon trees lost their blossom. In the fields, irrigation canals cut through the green and abundant grass where, scattered by shepherds who laughed as they beat them with their sticks, goats came to graze. Tall thin boys walked through the streets with their hands tucked inside their robes and women teased their husbands at nightfall. New spring, new fantasies, nature as men never cease to desire her. Ja'far was preparing himself for his marriage, but he had no illusions.

The caliph announced his return and that of his court. The palace became filled with bustling activity: the town grew feverish. When, when would the festivities be?

Completely hidden to men's eyes, princess Abassa returned to the caliph's palace on a camel amid cries of joy from the women lining the streets. Each one of them envied her. Did they not all thrill to think that she would share Ja'far's bed? For an instant, even the oldest among them rediscovered the enthusiasm of their youth and let out their joyous trills. A body, a mouth, such eyes, a gift from God, a gift from God . . . The camel swayed and the hidden princess listened to the cries all around as they all rejoiced at her happiness; slowness of the beast's steps, undulation of his back, a little boat – lost up there in a wind that was sweeping her where she didn't want to go; was she crying? Princess Abassa never cried.

The palace gate closed behind her, white walls on the coolness of the courtyard; for one fleeting moment, the image of a tomb came into my mind. I returned to my master.

'The princess is back,' I told him, 'the caliph returns tomorrow.'

Ja'far did not move. It was not fitting that he should go to the palace. He had to wait, but for what?

Harun and Ja'far's separation came to an end. They were back together, their bodies reunited; their love and their hate, so intricately entwined that they could no longer distinguish gentleness from violence, attraction from repulsion. Harun and Ja'far were drowning in each other, perhaps because they had lost their footing many years before and were now simply drifting helplessly. Their strength, their power and their riches, all these were like deep and turbulent waters, engulfing them. I thought of Ja'far eating and sleeping with the shepherds during our mad gallop towards Baghdad, of his torn coat, his dusty and bearded face, and I knew that he had never been so happy; never had he been so much in love. The fruit was full and ripe, ready to be picked or to rot, to be tasted or thrown away. Of a strong, wilful, courageous and idealistic man they had made a courtier. The suave odours of the palace had become sickly, and he no longer noticed. Fadl, who had remained pure and intransigent, had been cast aside. Ja'far had triumphed, but at his own expense. That evening, alone on the terrace above my master's apartments, I looked up at the sky. What had I been? Perhaps the only person who had really loved Ja'far al-Barmaki, the only one who had really been sincere. Abassa? Abassa wanted to win Ja'far for herself; she was taking him from her brother; she wanted to make him melt into her, so that his renown, his beauty, and all he represented in the empire, so that all these things would become her own. To make her brother's – the caliph's – lover, mad with love for her, what a victory for a girl of fifteen! Did she love him, this brother? It sometimes occurred to me that she hated him. And me, a simple servant, I prayed to God for that all-powerful caliph before whom the whole world bowed down and who was more alone than the Beduin lost in the immensity of the desert.

The marriage celebrations were decided upon. In May, Baghdad, like an exploding star, would sparkle in a shower of luminous rain, in a Greek fire which, to the very walls of Byzantium, of Samarkand, of Jerusalem and of Cordoba, would proclaim the splendours of the Abbasid court. In the four corners of the empire, in the shadow of the minarets, the community of Muslims would gather round storytellers to hear how, one fine week in spring, princess Abassa, of the Prophet's family, the sister of the caliph Harun al-Rashid, may God pro-tect him, had married Ja'far ben Yahya al-Barmaki, the Persian, the powerful vizier of immense riches and legendary beauty. They would speak of the music, the dances, the feasts, the wines, the sumptuous dresses, the jewels, the perfumes, the wild cavalcades, and children's eyes would open wide in wonder. But could they, these poor people, could they imagine the true splendour of those celebrations that lasted a whole week? In the days before the event, mules, camels and carts jostled together at the four gates of the city, at the gates of Kufa, Basra, Khurasan and Damas, all loaded with victuals of every kind for the meals that the caliph would be giving for the whole town, for the Golden Palace, where Harun's court would be feasting, and for Ja'far's residence, where he, his family and his friends would be celebrating the marriage. On the last day of the celebrations, on the last evening, the affianced would come together for the ultimate meal; Abassa would lift up her veil for Ja'far and everyone would depart, leaving them alone. How much time would Harun grant them? Five minutes, less perhaps. Ja'far did not want to think about it. He would see Abassa, whose face he had not beheld – except fleetingly during the hunt – for nearly three years. He had remembered it as a unique beauty and was burning with desire to contemplate it again.

On the eve of the first day, Baghdad sank into a feverish slumber. In their palaces, the two fiancés thought constantly of each other and could not sleep. At dawn, the silence was broken by the sound of flutes and tambourines; the celebrations were beginning. Singers and dancers invaded the squares. Tables had been set out and on them were served stews, bread, pastries and great bowls of curdled milk. Jugglers, fire eaters and acrobats vied with each other in skill to capture the attention of onlookers who seemed incapable of deciding where they should go next. The suqs were closed: the craftsmen, shopkeepers and apprentices were all out on the streets; groups formed and dispersed, women laughed together behind their veils and everywhere children were running about, grabbing bread or cakes on their way. In the evening, the streets were lit up. All around, thousands of oil lamps had been set out, and their flickering light cast uncertain smiles on to the façades of the houses – now joyous, now grimacing. For five whole days, people ate and drank until dawn.

In the caliph's palace, the women surrounded Abassa. Together, they feasted, laughed, dressed up in fine clothes, watched dances and listened to poems and love stories. The women looked at the princess with envy in their eyes, joking about her future pleasures and about the merits of her husband, which seemed immense to them. The princess listened to them; rarely did she laugh. People thought she was modest and took no notice. As each new day brought them closer to the nuptial night, their excitement grew even more intense; in graphic terms, they described to Abassa the thousand talents of her husband, and the young girl bowed her head. There was nothing to be said or done; she just had to wait. Aziza, who alone knew the truth, would sometimes take her hand and squeeze it in her own. On the eve of the last day, when the two of them were standing apart from the other women – the princess herself told Ja'far of this later – Aziza, as she was arranging the bride's tresses, murmured:

'Have hope, Abassa. I shall help you, but you must wait for the right moment, even if it is slow to come.'

Then, for the first time since the beginning of the festivities, Abassa showed signs of joy.

Harun celebrated the marriage of his favourite sister in the company of his relations and friends. During those five days he seemed perfectly happy and the magnificence of his hospitality overwhelmed everyone. Night and day were joined in a cortège of dances and feasts, of music and perfumes that turned people's heads just as much as the cool wine. The men spoke respectfully of the fiancée but their thoughts were bold; she was said to be so beautiful! Ja'far had found a royal gift in the caliph's bed.

In my master's palace, the opulence of the festivities was incredible. The Barmakids, wild with pride at this alliance, poured out the immensity of their fortune on their friends, parents, relations and clients. People drank from golden goblets and ate from vermeil dishes. Poets, storytellers and wise men charmed the guests during meals where as many as thirty courses were served. Arab, Persian and Greek were spoken. The most cultivated and refined minds in the empire were present. Alids and Sunnites together celebrated the fiancé – the dearest, most admired and most envied friend. Ja'far gave thanks, ate and drank with his friends and spoke of literature, poetry, arts, hunting and women, all with the same interest. He seemed happy. The envy he inspired left him indifferent. He was too noble to pride himself on his fortune and happiness. His fiancée was scarcely mentioned, unless with the greatest deference; his rank and nobility silenced the jokes normally made at weddings. These two young people were isolated by the respect that surrounded them, that fixed them in the coldness, the immobility and the beauty of those antique statues that are forever looking out on life from their empty eyes, stretching out petrified arms from their perfect bodies. Ja'far, magnificently dressed, his astonishing face framed by a white kuffiya, at times seemed almost dead in his perfection. But then he would smile, and the magic charm would work its spell, spreading life, youth and sensuality all around him. During those five days, he hardly slept; I stood beside him and we spoke together. Not of Abassa, never, but of our youth, our follies, of Syria, of the feasts in the caliph's palace, of political matters, of literature, of sciences and of death. My master, who was a pious man, did not believe in paradise. On the eve of the last day, the day when his fiancée would at last be brought to him, he asked me: 'Why do you love me, Ahmed? Our paths have been so different since our youth. We are both thirty-five and I have never seen anyone else at your side but me, neither woman nor man. Why?'

I had been waiting for this question for such a long time. What good would it do to be silent now? I had known the answer for years.

'My lord, from birth onwards, each man carries within himself a capital of aspirations and dreams. All his life he will seek to spend this capital, to spread it about him – giving it to others in the hope that he will receive himself back in exchange and thus, little by little, rebuild himself, until the edifice is secure and the hour of death has come. You sought yourself in your concubines, in Harun, and now in Abassa. Your image is being built up, piece by piece, each one being a little part of you. As for me, I found everything in one single moment, when I knew that I loved you. I was re-created, complete, ready to die. God has granted me this privilege, not to wander, not to implore, not to regret. I am nothing and I am everything, a perfectly rounded sphere, a closed world, a golden orange of which you are the other half. Nothing can complete me, nothing can finish me: I am, and it is well thus. My only demand, my only desire, is that you should hold this globe in your hands, that you should warm it and that your face should be reflected in it.'

Ja'far looked at me for a long moment without speaking, then he took my hand.

'You are lucky, Ahmed, you are both small and immense at the same time, and I, who hold you in my hands, I would like to become smooth and serene, in your image, whereas I am in turmoil like a heart that beats too strongly. I have everything and yet I would have much more.'

I clasped his hand in mine. That night we were close to one another.

'My lord, allow me to recite a passage from the Qur'an which has come into my mind:

Your obsession with desire grows and grows until you
descend into your tombs.
But you will come to know! If only you knew with true
knowledge you would surely see your hell.
When the time comes, assuredly, you will see with the
eye of certainty.
And on that day, it will be asked of you what you have
done with the gift of life.'

Ja'far said nothing. This decisive answer left him bemused, pensive. Finally, he got up, asked me for something to drink and said simply: 'I have the premonition that I shall soon see all these things very clearly. Go, Ahmed, go, I am thirsty and tomorrow is an important day.'

At dawn the next day began the last and most lavish of the celebrations; when Ja'far would send for his wife and have her brought to his house. In the caliph's palace, Abassa, like an obedient doll, let herself be bathed, plucked, perfumed and massaged by her women. They dressed her hair, giving her long curly locks a good brushing before pouring sweet-smelling salts on them: they made her up, surrounding her eyes with kohl and painting her cheeks and her mouth. Her hands and feet were dyed with henna until they became brown. Then, carried by two slaves, the arrival of the heavy dress – woven entirely of gold thread and encrusted with sapphires in Ja'far's colours, the golden babouches, the veil of transparent black silk, spangled with pearls and golden medallions, and the black mask, also fastened behind the head with gold threads. Two other servants brought a chain of gold and sapphires for the forehead, long earrings encrusted with diamonds, pearl necklaces, a golden belt, and countless bracelets for the wrists and ankles. Set against the fragility of the princess, this jewellery seemed out of place, crushing, heavy, and made her seem more frail and even smaller, a bird-woman caught in a gold net. She did not move. Was she thinking that, though meticulously, sensually prepared for the pleasure of a man, ready to be warm, moist, soft and sweet-smelling in his arms, under his hand and against his body – she would nevertheless find herself alone that night, consumed by the desire for the man – her husband – that she would not even be able to approach? Or was she thinking that she would be his at last? Her impassive face gave nothing away.

In the women's chamber, the long day pursued its course. Abassa was now set on a ceremonial, throne-like bed, and for hours women filed past her to admire her and pay her compliments. The heat was stifling. One slave fanned the little bride, another brought her something to drink. Her skin was glistening underneath the excessive make-up, under the thick, hot dress; but she did not move and offered herself to these eyes and to their covetousness with a detachment that resembled indifference.

At midday, when everyone had admired the bride, a meal was served, but the women, encased in their ceremonial dresses, barely touched it. From this moment, all attention, all desire was focused on the arrival of the cortège which would come from Ja'far's palace to fetch Abassa. The youngest ran to the windows, the oldest listened for the noises from the main courtyard. They nibbled at fruits and cakes, leaving them almost untouched. Were the horses ready? The camels, and the servants? Would they be at their best during the short journey between the two palaces? Several would be going into the outside world for the first time in years; the captive birds beat against the walls, blinded by the dazzling light.

At last, a noise was heard, rising from the courtyard to the women's apartments. The cortège was arriving, the cortège was there! Abassa, who had been dozing, stretched out on the cushions, overpowered by the heat, was made to get up. Quickly, they arranged her veil, and straightened her clothes. The cotton mask was put on and more rouge was applied to her lips and cheekbones, black around her eyes, and amber and jasmine about her neck, behind her ears and at the bend of her wrists. Her women gathered round her, standing behind the bride's mother, her aunts, her cousins, and the two queens, Zubaydah and Aziza – the Arab and the Persian, side by side for the first time. A eunuch opened the door; the ladies could go down. Old Yahya himself had come to fetch his future daughter. With his son, Fadl al-Barmaki, and with his relatives and friends, he was waiting for her at the bottom of the great staircase.

Abassa descended slowly, her head high, at once both stiff and supple, like a young stem that the summer has yet to load with fruit. The chin, the full fleshy mouth, the long slim neck, the henna-browned hands, the slowness of her movements and the fire of her eyes; these were the only features discernible amid all the gold, sapphires and pearls. Under the carapace of metal, cloth and precious stones, burnt the ardour of a passion that she could never subdue. Coldness of a woman whose body was seized with trembling at the thought of the man she was about to be with; quivering of the mouth, imperfect stillness of hands that tingled with the desire to dance on the lover's skin. Abassa was descending. The flutes, tambourines and citharas were playing, their music was sensual, obsessive, joyous; revels for the gift of a body.

Following the Barmakids, she blinked in the courtyard at the sinking sun whose gold wove itself into that of her finery. A white horse was waiting for her, harnessed with silver and pearls. Two black servants helped her mount and, on each side of the embroidered saddle, between the pantaloons and the babouches, could be seen her braceleted ankles. Harun was there with his family, and they bowed to the bride. Then Muhammad, the caliph's personal slave, dressed in black, took the horse's bridle and two horsemen carrying the standard of the Abbasids took their places on either side of the princess. They set off. With Yahya and Fadl beside him, the caliph walked behind his sister; then came the closest relatives, some servants and some musicians. They left the palace. The streets were festooned with palms and flowers and lined with crowds. The triumphal cheers from the women on the terraces drowned out the tambourines and wind instruments. The sun was setting and, against the softness of dusk, the clamour accompanying the princess seemed febrile, violent and wild.

Abassa advanced, looking neither right nor left, her eyes set on her fiancé's palace; that sumptuous residence where she was going for the first time. Was she aware of the fever all around her, that sensual expectation that made all the people of Baghdad quiver with excitement and which, that night, would make them embrace in the darkness of their chambers?

The cortège crossed the river after passing through the quarter of the Barmakids at Shamassiya. Ja'far's palace rose up before them; vast, simple, superb, surrounded by high crenellated walls of clay. Guards, dressed all in black and blue, surrounded the gate, their sabres in their hands. The cedar-sculpted double doors were wide open. The procession entered the courtyard with its white marble paving and with the orange trees in their boxes all around its sides. The horses' hooves trod the blue and green mosaic and rounded the basin that had been built there, being sprayed as they passed by the two jets of water that gushed from the mouths of the black marble dolphins. A few steps away, behind the colonnade that girt the courtyard – upright, motionless, clothed in blue, silver and black – Ja'far was waiting for his bride. The princess's horse stopped and their eyes met for a few seconds – an eternity; their breath was short, their chests heavy, emptied. Then my master went to greet the caliph, took his hand, and kissed it. The women led Abassa to the guest chamber.

The ceremony started up anew with processions and congratulations; Abassa, upright as ever, was waiting. The servants busied themselves to prepare the meal. Then entered Ja'far's aunt, the sister of his dead mother; majestic, opulent in a robe of scarlet and gold brocade. In her hand she held a vermeil tray and, on this tray, a simple, round cake, glistening with honey. She stopped in front of her future niece, broke the cake, and, three times over, made her eat a piece out of her hand. From now on, Abassa was a Barmakid. They formed a circle around her. Ja'far approached and stopped a few steps away. They were standing opposite each other. Joyous music burst out. People murmured; they were waiting. Finally, after exchanging glances with the caliph, who nodded his head, the little princess, still standing, lifted her hands to her mask. She was not trembling. Her eyes never left Ja'far's. Pushing away the help of a servant woman, her fingers untied the golden fastenings fixed behind the veil. She remained in this position for a few seconds and then, without hesitation, withdrew the mask. The room was filled with cheering and deafening music. Abassa and Ja'far exchanged intent gazes, almost as if they were alone. Ja'far saw the delicate face, the fine straight nose, the round cheeks of a preserved childhood, the sensual mouth, the chin, and that face of which he had so often dreamed was now uncovered before him. He wanted to stretch out his hand, to caress it, and he could do nothing. Abassa contemplated her husband – his hair, his eyes, his mouth, his body, everything that would from now on be the object of her life. Time had stopped; they were there, together, like birds hanging in the evening breeze, in the silence of an immensity. They took the princess by the arm. She shuddered; it was time for the meal – in the women's apartment for the women, in the guest chamber for the men. Then it would be time for the guests to leave. The couple would be left alone for their night of eternity.

The Barmakids gave a magnificent banquet for this nuptial meal. The caliph, who was honouring their house with his presence, stayed close by Ja'far, smiling and peaceful. What had he decided? What had he planned? I could discover nothing of this. He ate and jested with his hosts, and only his eyes, which settled from time to time on Ja'far, hinted at a slight tension, an emotion I could not define. It was growing late. The guests, lying on cushions, intoxicated with music, food and wine, stayed to talk or doze. They were waiting for the caliph to rise. The women, on their side, were waiting for the end of the men's meal in the guest chamber so that they could part company with the bride, leave her in the chamber, alone, waiting for her husband. At last, Harun rose and was immediately followed by Ja'far and all the guests. He gave his hand to Yahya, and the old man kissed it; then, taking my master by the arm, he took him aside. I was close by.

'I will wait for you tonight in my palace, Ja'far, for I have hardly seen you this last week. Do not delay. I wish we were already together.'

And, when my master, who was pale and still, made no reply, he added:

'Be discreet. It would be unwise to let it be known that you were abandoning your young wife. Muhammad, my slave, will stay with you. He will go with you to ward off any undesirable meetings in the streets of Baghdad. These celebrations have attracted the local scum. May God watch over you!'

And, casting his eyes over the banqueters, he left.

The guests rose in their turn and took their leave. Ja'far remained behind, alone with his father and brother.

'Come,' said Fadl, 'I shall take you to your wife. She is waiting for you.'

They arrived at the door, followed by the caliph's slave. Fadl bowed and left, Ja'far entered; the servant stayed at the door – silent, impassive, perfectly impenetrable. He had his orders and would execute them without passion, scrupulously. Standing before a vast bed covered with cushions and draperies, Abassa was waiting. They had removed her robe and jewels; they had dressed her hair and clothed her in a simple white galabiya. She watched her husband as he came to her. Then, suddenly – was it the emotion, the fatigue, the nervous tension? – she burst into tears. My master was beside her, he opened his arms and she pressed herself against his breast, against the thick embroidered tunic that scratched her skin. For a few moments they remained thus, nestling close to each other, then she looked up at him and Ja'far timidly caressed her eyes, her cheeks, her mouth. Abassa murmured:

'How much time do we have?'

'I don't know. Muhammad is just behind the door. He is waiting for me.'

They were both trembling. They no longer knew what to do or say in this brief instant that had been granted them. Their impatience clashed against their certainty that the slave would knock at the door at any moment. Then, Abassa wrapped her arms round Ja'far's neck, rose up on tiptoe, and took her husband's mouth. My master quivered, his hands grew frantic – then, as if he sensed what was happening, the slave knocked on the door.

'Make haste, my lord, the caliph is waiting for us.'

Ja'far, my master, the courageous, the proud, the arrogant . . . Ja'far let out a sob and pushed away his wife.

'May God protect us, Abassa, I have to go.'

Three steps away from him, Abassa stared at her husband with frantic eyes.

'I will be yours, Ja'far, soon. I will let you know when the time comes.'

Muhammad gave another knock.

'Go and open up, Ahmed,' Ja'far ordered me, 'and tell him I am coming.'

He took one last look at his wife and went out. The caliph was waiting for him on his wedding night, waiting for Ja'far to thank him for this poisoned gift that left a terrible bitterness in his mouth.

At dawn we returned to my master's house. Abassa was no longer there. Two servants had taken her to the Golden Palace where, from now on, she was going to live. Was this not the proper place for a royal princess? Ja'far said nothing but, without taking any rest, he left to go hunting in the east, in the mountains, and he only came back three days later.

AHMED'S NINTH NIGHT

The wind had fallen, but the heat remained oppressive and heavy with thunder. Would God's beneficial rain come and wash the city, refresh the fields, send quivers through the animals, the languid camels, the lean cows, the wandering goats? Tomorrow, perhaps, or the day after, or later, much later. In the drowsy lull of summer, time no longer mattered, or almost; a kind of peace, crushing and humid, made bodies still and minds calm. Neighbours no longer quarrelled, children played peacefully in the shade and the old men spoke monologues in the half light of the suqs or mosques. Life began only at night, when the fires in the streets and houses leapt up towards the sky and lit up the stars. From terrace to terrace, friends called to each other and paid each other visits, and the great square grew bright with words and gestures, smells and memories. Ahmed, where was Ahmed? The night before, so few people had heard him and yet now they all wanted to know, to travel back into the past, to return to the glorious days when power was throned in Baghdad, when the whole world was dazzled by the splendours of the round town. Children searched but could not find him. No one knew if he had a house, so where should they look? Here or there, on a street corner, in the depth of some courtyard, or near a fountain? Another storyteller tried in vain to capture the people's attention, but that night Ahmed was truly the only source for those dreams where each desired to slake his thirst. One man suggested that they go and look on the bridge where Ahmed's memories must unfailingly lead him, but he was not there. So, where else should they look? Had he not perhaps died like a dog on a street corner, as if crushed by the southern wind? Had he fallen asleep in the world of his memory, taken refuge in his past? Suddenly, an old man stepped forward. He knew, yes, he knew where Ahmed was; he had often seen him huddled up, far from here, in the western quarter, beyond the river, in front of the high cedarwood gate of a vast abandoned house, Ja'far's palace, the one of which the caliph Al-Mamun had since taken possession and which was now open to the four winds of the world's forgetfulness. Could some young man ride there on an ass and bring him back? Then, a tall and svelte young boy stepped forward, his handsome face framed by a turban; he knew the Persian quarter well, for he lived there. A trader lent him his mule and he set off at a trot, his slim legs on either side of the animal showing naked through the galabiya. To pass the time, people talked of business or of their families and nibbled a few cakes or a few dates – the women on one side and the men on the other. Those who had been present the night before retold Ja'far's story, but the words were not the same, the emotion was absent. From time to time, a child would run to the end of a street to see if he was coming and return, making great gestures: no, there was no one. At last, from the end of a narrow passage in the spice-sellers' suq, the trot of a mule could be heard. The young Persian emerged and, hidden behind him, hanging on to his waist, old Ahmed, whose head was nodding gently to each side. In front of the now opening circle, the mule stopped and the young man jumped to the ground, taking the old man in his arms like a limp and lightweight corn dolly. Ahmed's eyes were shut and his head was still nodding; he was mute, his lips closed over his toothless mouth. They sat him down with his back to the wall, as usual, and placed his stick beside him.

'Do you want something to drink?' asked the young man.

Ahmed acquiesced with a movement of his chin. Someone went to fetch him a goblet of cool fresh water; he drank it, then opened his eyes and looked at all the people who had gathered around him.

'Why are you here tonight?' he asked.

'To listen to you, old man,' came the reply from all around, 'to hear your story.'

Ahmed nodded.

'Yes, my story. It won't take much longer. I must make haste, for my life is fading like a lamp. Yesterday's wind blew on it and reduced it to a mere glow . . . I had fallen asleep near my master's palace – I often go back there to converse with him and talk about the business of life – and so it was that this sleep would not let me go, but left me prostrate on the ground. This young man came and I followed him. I must get it finished now before I fall asleep once more, yes, I must finish what I have begun, my mouth must release Ja'far, who is locked up inside me, before I smother him with my own death. Free, he will do as God wills. We are all in His hands.'

Ahmed was silent for an instant; he drank another mouthful of water, and lifted his eyes to the heavens.

See how our summer is hot, torrid. The summer of 185 [801AD] was the same. From June onwards, the air in the street, like a steam bath, made faces glisten and bodies perspire. People went out only at night, when they would sleep on the terraces or, in rich households, around the basins of inner gardens, where the music of the water refreshes dreams and calms the body. Ja'far, Abassa and Harun saw each other almost every day. The princess now left her face uncovered when she was with her brother and her husband. Sometimes she would eat with them. Most often, she would join them on the patio in the evening for a game of dice or chess, or to listen to music and poetry. Deferential with the caliph, she was distant with Ja'far, avoiding contact with him, trying not to look at him. When, at dice, their fingers brushed, she would immediately snatch her hand away and Harun, observing her, would laugh. He caressed my master in front of his sister less often now, but all his behaviour showed clearly that he considered himself in total possession of him. As for Ja'far, his rancour against Harun was so tangled up with his desire that he no longer knew which was stronger. One fed the other.

Ramadan came in July that year, and sleep descended on the court; no more festivities, no more banquets. Abassa liked to walk alone in the gardens at sunrise before returning home and waiting for the night. Her slight silhouette would come and go between the flower-beds, would sit on the edge of the basin and dangle its fingers there; or, as if contemplating herself in her own mirror, she would spend hours watching the birds in the aviary. During the month of fasting, Ja'far hardly ever came to the palace. Each day he would send her a message, which I carried myself. Once, once only, in the main garden, where she was followed by a tame gazelle that refused to leave her, I saw the princess cry as she took the letter. She did not open it.

'What use are words,' she said, 'when the mouth that utters them and the hand that writes them are forever away from me.'

'Forever does not exist, princess Abassa. You are dearer to my master than his own eyes; why then should he not one day find a way of proving it to you?'

Abassa stopped, and put her arm round the gazelle's neck.

'Yes, perhaps, but tell him to hurry, Ahmed, for I am beginning to feel lost waiting for him and my courage is deserting me. I shall not survive a year without him.'

I looked at her. She was hidden behind her mask, but her eyes were so expressive that she was as if uncovered before me.

'Princess, my master does not dare to try anything for fear of harming you, but on the smallest sign from yourself he will run to you.'

'Then tell him, Ahmed, to be ready; if I am to die, then I would prefer to have been his wife first.'

I could not help laughing.

'Princess Abassa, nobody dies at the age of fifteen.'

Her eyes became clouded with anger, and with a single movement she pushed away the gazelle.

'Do you believe that? Then you have never loved!'

We stared at each other for an instant without speaking. Seeing in my eyes that she had hurt me, she smiled and put her hand on my arm.

'Tell Ja'far that I shall call him soon and that, whatever I decide, he must obey me.'

I bowed and left her. At the end of the alley I turned around. She was sitting on the edge of the basin and reading the letter from her husband. She was crying no longer.

The festivities at the end of Ramadan were joyous. In spite of the heat, people danced, shared mutton and cakes and came out on to the streets. At the Golden Palace a great feast was held and to it came Ja'far and all his family. Yahya and Fadl had understood that my master's brilliant marriage was a trap but had never spoken of it and, to all the clients and friends who asked for news of the bride, they replied that her health was perfect and that the young couple were extremely happy together.

For the celebration, Harun himself led the great prayer

in the mosque. It was packed; the women went to the area reserved for them and the men assembled in the prayer room. The caliph's family was present, as were the Barmakids; they stood side by side but separate. Fadl al-Rabi turned away when his eyes met Ja'far's; his round and self-satisfied face showed that he was not afraid of him.

Contemplative yet excited atmosphere of prayer, rustling of clothes brushing against the marble tiles, greenish half-light that made the air like still lake water. On the blue and white faience tiles, the caliph led the prayer and, under the hundreds of oil lamps hidden in globes of crystal, each person watched him and followed his gestures. The echo of the prayer expired against the bronze door of the mosque, against the cedarwood screen behind which the women were praying, on the carpets where naked feet stood and slipped; and the heat itself was held back outside the building's thick walls. It was cool.

In the evening, Aziza held a reception in her chambers: it was the first celebration she had given and Harun rejoiced to see her less withdrawn, less reserved. He still loved her tenderly and she had just given birth to her third child, a daughter. The second crown price, Al-Mamun, was at her side, a small boy with lively eyes and a tender heart that delighted his father, his tutor and all those who came near him. Hidden behind a mask embroidered with silver thread, marvellously decked out in all the jewels the caliph had given her, Aziza welcomed her guests. Though her figure was ample now, she was still beautiful, and her green eyes, set off by her emeralds which dangled from her ears and curled around her neck and wrists, seemed to be looking through her guests in search of another, expected long since.

At last, Abassa entered and, behind her came her

husband Ja'far, Harun and queen Zubaydah, who was leading by the hand al-Amin, thin and dark in his embroidered galabiya. By speaking to him in contemptuous tones of the Persian woman and her sons, his mother had made him into a distrustful, haughty, vain creature. And such he would remain for the rest of his short life.

Aziza rose for Abassa and greeted her; the men formed a group in the corner of the chamber and talked of hunting, falcons and horses; the women, masked or veiled, laughed softly, reaching out to the trays of cakes, admiring each other's jewels and embroidered dresses. With a natural gesture, Aziza took Abassa's arm and led her to a corner where they were alone. The caliph, who had his back turned, did not see them. The princess spoke quickly and in such a soft voice that the young girl had to come very close to her. They were standing up against each other, and could feel each other's warm breath.

'Princess Abassa, listen to me, and do not interrupt me, for time is short. My aunt, may God protect her, lives very close to the palace, in a modest house on the edge of the draper's quarter. She came to visit me recently and I asked her to give such a proof of devotion that it might even cost her her life. She accepted. This woman is like a mother to me. I asked her to open her door without asking any questions to one of my woman friends who had need of her, that she might receive a man there, and I told her that if this were known we would all die. She manifested no curiosity. She will do it. During your absence, I shall detain Harun, but never be out of the palace for too long. You will go in modest apparel, like a servant; the guard will let you back in – he has been given gold. He does not know, and will not try to find out why one of my women will return to the palace at night. It is he who will be on duty over the coming month: after that, we shall see. During this feast that I am giving on your behalf, you are going to tell Ja'far what I have arranged; he will give me a sign of agreement if he approves my plan and then I will warn my aunt and, as from tomorrow, her door will be open. Go now and talk to your husband.'

Abassa took the princess's hand – she did not dare kiss it for fear of attention – and stepped back. Her eyes were extraordinarily bright. I was close to her, but she felt no distrust towards me.

'Why are you doing this, Aziza? I do not know, but may God bless you for your help.'

'But Abassa, I am a Persian myself and I owe my happiness to Ja'far. I know he loves you, may God watch over you both!'

The princess made off, joined Zubaydah and conversed with her for an instant – they were relatives and saw each other in spite of the queen's hatred for Ja'far – then she stood aside for a while, glancing from time to time at Aziza, who was approaching Harun. The caliph turned towards the princess and she kissed his hand. Having watched them for a moment, Abassa went to her husband, greeted him and, in an undertone, as if they were talking of things without importance, and without their eyes meeting even once, she reported what Aziza had said. Ja'far started, his eyes lit up, but his body did not move. His father was approaching, so the princess withdrew.

Time had become a poem, a love song, exquisite music, an unending prayer. Ja'far gazed through the window at the sky. He wanted to melt into it and, like it, to be luminous, limitless, light and fluid. He closed his eyes. He, Ja'far ben Yahya al-Barmaki, was invincible; the following day he would possess the missing keystone to the edifice of his happiness: he would press the body of a royal princess against his own, possess her, become her. Princess Abassa's heart was beating so strongly that she had to sit down and she was so pale that a woman came to ask her if she was not unwell. Joy and anxiety stifled her. Tomorrow she would be a woman, tomorrow the man she loved would see her naked, offered up in the yellow lamplight. Tomorrow she would possess his mouth, his saliva, his body. She would caress his skin. She would feel him, alive inside her. God, how suffocated she felt! Why, why then?

Ja'far left the group of men and went up to Aziza.

'I thank you, princess, for your hospitality. I must return to my palace, and the image of your beauty and your nobility will go with me there.'

He bowed, backed away and, before turning to leave, looked straight at her and nodded his consent.

Aziza had seen it. She turned away and joined Harun, who was also taking his leave. He desired to spend the night with the princess and had not detained Ja'far.

Side by side on our horses, we returned to the palace. I was worried.

'What will you do if the caliph calls for you tomorrow night? Will he not find it strange that Abassa and yourself are absent?'

Ja'far was smiling.

'Ahmed, if it were a matter of being reunited with the one you love, would you do it?'

'Certainly, master, I would do it, but I am only a servant and the risk I would be taking would be small. It is not the same for you.'

'Do you believe, Ahmed, that my dependence on the caliph is as great as all that? Do you really believe that my power is as nothing against his?'

'Against the caliph, master, no man may rebel: you

may be a proud, noble, ardent stallion and you can gallop to the ends of the earth, but you cannot throw him.'

'Princess Aziza is helping us, Ahmed, she will manage to detain the caliph; she will know how to make his night long and his suspicion short. Twilight and dawn will meet like a crown about our heads, and Abassa will be in the palace even when the warmth of the princess is once again wrapping itself around Harun's body. I know him.'

I dismounted and took the bridle of his horse.

'May this night be brief for you, my lord, and the following night infinite. I shall accompany you to the house of the princess's aunt and shall kill with my own hands whosoever desires to penetrate into that house, even if it is the caliph in person who desires to enter. I wish you a peaceful night, my lord. I will sleep in front of your door.'

What did we do the next day? I do not know. My memory has retained neither the words nor the gestures that we exchanged, Ja'far and I, no doubt because we were happy to let the hours go by like the flight of the grouse above the desert in the first days of autumn. A brushing noise, a movement of light and wind, a crossing.

Ja'far went to the caliph's palace, sat on the Council and shared the caliph's evening meal. Night was shadowing the gardens, the rosery and the patio with its murmuring fountain. The flowers that are the stars scattered themselves, bouquets of umbels in the bottomless vase of the infinite. Little by little, the heat was drowning in space, as it opened itself to the tenderness of the evening like a shellfish offering its valves to the caress of the sea.

Repeating the call to prayer from one minaret to another, the muezzins called out their great hopes. Ja'far and Harun bowed towards the Holy City, their arms and their shoulders touched, but that night their hearts were not beating together, a wave parted them from each other, carrying them to faraway shores where different women awaited them – a Persian for the Arab, an Arab for the Persian. Perfect symmetry even in their very difference. I thought of these two men, so near and yet so distant from each other: the Arab born in Persia, the Persian born in Medina, all their life together would have been the confluence of these two rivers.

The caliph and my master played a game of dice on the patio. The cicadas were humming, a few night birds called to each other in the twilight of the attics and towers. It was already late.

'Do you want me tonight?' asked Ja'far.

And, tenderly, he took Harun's hand and held it in his own. The caliph smiled.

'My beautiful Ja'far, this night is your own, for I am going to be unfaithful to you once again.'

'Unfaithful, Imam?'

Harun laughed, his clear laughter was without ambiguity.

'Yes, unfaithful, my brother, but with the woman you gave me, with princess Aziza. I feel great tenderness and great desire for her at the present time. If God wills it, we will soon have another little prince.'

He rose and gave his hand to be kissed. My master bowed.

'Until tomorrow, then, my lord, perhaps by the evening I shall have succeeded in reconquering your desire!'

'Do not doubt it, Ja'far; I wish you a good night.'

My master went out slowly. I followed him, but once he was in the main courtyard and a servant had brought him his horse, I saw that his hands were trembling.

'Let us go, Ahmed,' he said, 'princess Abassa must be waiting for me.'

He was pale. I could almost hear his heart beating.

We returned to Ja'far's palace. We had to be seen entering and leave our horses in the stables, then go out again, secretly. My master would go up to his apartments, make it known that he did not want to be disturbed and then leave the palace with me via the terraces and gardens. It must have been around midnight; everything was calm. We passed some guards and a few servants, and they greeted us. Ja'far went on, peaceful and august. Behind him, I closed the door to his apartments, with its painted golden leaves. Then, in a trice, my master rid himself of his court abaya, his kuffiya and his galabiya. I handed him a simple robe of grey cloth with a belt and wrapped a white turban around his hair. As a precaution, he took a dagger which he hid in a pocket of his robe and, without leaving me the time to change my sandals, we set off. Ja'far was laughing: at the age of thirty he was running across the terraces like an adolescent going to meet a woman, and this escapade, his disguise – everything aroused his desire, made him mad, juvenile and joyous.

Above our heads the sky was clear, the waxing moon was giving out an opaque and incandescent breath which caressed the stars. A few dogs were barking and, somewhere below, far down on a terrace, the jangle of a tambourine was heard. The peace of evening was over Baghdad.

We walked up a few deserted alleyways where the odours of spice and tannin still hung in the air. At the corner of a fountain, an old beggar sat dozing. Ja'far put a gold coin on his robe. 'May God be with you!' murmured the man. And Ja'far glanced at me. Yes, pray God that He would be with him!

The drapers' suq was deserted. The workshops were closed. We walked silently up the main street. Right at the end, at the corner of an arched passageway, a little ochre house. To enter, we had to descend a few steps. The door was of wood; the windows were tiny, protected by wrought-iron bars. Do not try to find this house, it exists only in my memory. It was consumed in a fire, a sudden, unpredictable fire, many years ago, a few months after my master's death. The old woman who lived there perished in the flames; an unfortunate accident, yes, a terrible misfortune. On the ashes the caliph built a madrasa where the children of the neighbourhood now untiringly repeat the holy words. Divine words efface human actions, hope abolishes memories. When I wander in this neighbourhood I see neither fire nor death nor vengeance; I feel happy and I love to hear the children recite the Holy Scripture. I sit down and I stay listening to them until the moment when the memory of those nights makes my ears deaf. Then the images of the past flood back and, so as not to offend God, I go.

The door had a wrought-iron knocker in the shape of a hand. Ja'far knocked. A young servant woman came to let us in and behind her we saw Aziza's aunt, wrapped in her chador.

'Come in, quickly,' she said, 'don't make any noise.'

She spoke in Persian. Her voice was slightly husky, sensual.

'The young woman is waiting for you.'

I wanted to stay downstairs.

'Come up,' said Ja'far, 'I would like you to stay in front of the door in order to warn me if there is the slightest danger.' The staircase was narrow: fleetingly, I thought back to our first visit to the home of Aziza's parents. Was Ja'far thinking of it too?

The old woman went before us, her small black form light and silent, the incarnation of destiny or death.

She drew back a red cotton curtain woven with white geometrical motifs.

'It's here,' was all she said. And, bending to go through – for the door was low – Ja'far entered.

I saw Abassa standing in the stagnant light of an oil lamp. She was wearing a simple white linen tunic which showed her bare arms. Her hair was loose and she was barefoot. She watched Ja'far come in. She was breathing quickly and her eyes were shining. Ja'far stopped, his tall silhouette filled the doorway. The curtain swung back behind him. Before turning away, I saw Abassa, with one gesture, remove her robe, and I saw Ja'far fall to his knees before her. Her slender young girl's body was fragile and delicate. She had small round breasts, a tiny waist, and long slim thighs and legs. Her abundant mane of curly brown hair came down to her hips. On her wrists and ankles she was wearing bracelets which shone in the light of the lamp. Ja'far had enfolded her in his arms and she was saying nothing. Her head slightly to one side, she put her hands on my master's turban, took it off, and gently stroked his curly hair.

I saw and heard nothing more. From time to time a dog barking, a conversation in the street or the noise of our hostess's footsteps on the ground floor of the house. One by one, the noises disappeared. It was late at night. I stayed on my feet – attentive, vigilant, lit by the light from the oil lamp behind the curtain, whence came only a few breaths or murmurings; or was it the night wind?

A few cocks crowed. I had been dozing on my feet and started. No noise was coming from behind the curtain now. It was time for us to go. In the daytime, Ja'far's clients and friends came to his apartments to discuss business and ask advice. He had to be there. The eyes and ears of the caliph were everywhere.

'Master,' I said, without lifting the curtain, 'day is near.' There was no answer.

'Master,' I repeated, and drew back the curtain.

Ja'far and Abassa were lying there naked, united in their embrace, and seemed to be asleep. The princess's hair covered my master's chest and shoulders. Their legs were entwined, their arms interlaced, and their faces were so close that their lips were almost touching. They were so beautiful that I could not bear to look at them.

Louder now, I called: 'Master, we must go.'

Ja'far started, gently disengaged himself from the princess and stood up. There were rings about his eyes and his mouth was swollen. As soon as he was awake, he looked at Abassa and smiled. She in her turn got up and put her arms around him. Then, in front of me, their mouths joined once again and their bodies came together. I saw my master strain towards the princess, like a mehara's neck towards a mirage of water. And she, moist and warm, was waiting for him, to quench the thirst of this traveller on his endless journey.

I stood there, gazing at them. My body, too, felt itself drawn towards them, towards that beauty which I beheld, and which made me tremble. So as to see them no longer, I put my head in my hands, stepped back and went out.

The old woman was on her way upstairs.

'Dawn is near,' she murmured, 'tell your master that he must leave. In a few instants the street will grow busy and he must not be seen. The slightest delay would be a great imprudence.'

I called once more.

'My lord, the night is drawing to an end. For the sake of the princess, you must leave.'

Ja'far had heard me. There was a noise in the room, the

rustling of clothes being slipped on. He drew back the curtain. His features seemed set, his eyes absent. Behind him I saw the princess, who was also getting dressed.

'Let us go, Ahmed,' he said.

He did not turn around, and we left. The return journey, amid the barking of the dogs and the crowing of the cocks, seemed short. My master was silent. Near the palace, as we were crossing the terraces of the stables, Ja'far seemed to emerge from a dream. His features grew animated and his eyes came alive. We jumped on to a terrace below us which looked over the vegetable gardens.

'Ahmed,' he said to me, and his eyes were burning, 'Ahmed, there is an eternity in man!'

We reached the bottom with one jump. My master had pulled his turban down over his face so as not to be recognised. In front of the stables, he stopped.

'Ahmed, saddle my horse.'

'Your horse, my lord! But are you not returning to your apartments?'

'I want to gallop, to gallop out into the distance. This morning, you see, I could not bear any constraint. I feel like a falcon called by the wind. Hurry!'

I tried to reason with him:

'Are you not supposed to be receiving your father and your cousins?'

Ja'far grew impatient.

'Go on, Ahmed, tell them I have gone hunting, tell them not to wait for me.'

'Shall I not go with you, my lord?'

'No, Ahmed, I want to be alone.'

I bowed. It was the first time my master had refused me. I went to saddle his horse. Ja'far was hot, he was tired out, but he felt an almost supernatural strength. He jumped into his saddle, dug his heels into his horse, making it rear up, then, letting out a great guttural yell of warlike triumph, he shot forward.

I saw him again only in the evening. He had eaten and slept with the Beduins. His face was calm, happy. Peace was upon him and in him. He held in his hands a little Arab princess, a smooth amber pearl, sensual, soothing, whose powerful perfume intoxicated him; Ja'far had reached a shore, limit of the world or of life. He was going to lay himself down there and enjoy his happiness. Nothing else mattered now.

That night he was at the caliph's palace. His happiness made him extraordinarily warm towards Harun. Harun's sister, his last most protected possession, belonged to him, he had made her a woman, he had possessed her as he had possessed her brother, and he felt strong, great, invincible. His power, his fortune, his seduction, all these things made him the most powerful man in the empire, and when he looked towards the caliph, he no longer lowered his eyes. Why should he?

Harun and Ja'far played at dice until dawn. Abassa did not come. To the caliph, who had asked for news of his sister, they replied that the princess, fatigued by the heat, was resting. Towards morning, Harun took some rest and desired that Ja'far remain with him. My master watched him as he slept. He was smiling.

At the end of the afternoon, as they were leaving the Council, Ja'far asked the caliph:

'Imam, will you allow me to visit my wife in her apartments?'

'Go,' replied Harun, 'and give her my greetings. Tell her that it should please me if she were here with us tonight.'

My master and I were announced at the princess's apartments. What risk was there? We would not be alone for one moment, and the caliph knew it. One of Abassa's women came to tell us that she was walking in her gardens. A servant had gone to announce our presence. We would have to wait. A Sudanese child came running in. She was laughing and her teeth sparkled like nacreous beads against the black pearl of her face.

'The princess is waiting for her husband in the rose garden near the little basin.'

We crossed a small courtyard planted with orange trees where water flowed in a shell-shaped basin of pink marble; then, a garden shaded by olive and almond trees, where lilies and ferns flowered around small stone walls climbed by stocks and sweet peas. Finally, through an arched door, half open, we caught sight of the rose garden and, at the very end, the basin where the princess bred the rarest and most colourful ducks – mallards, teals, pintails and mandarins. She came to see them often, and would sometimes speak to them and give them food. The path was sanded and muffled the sound of our steps.

Abassa had her back towards us. Flanked by two servants, she was leaning over the basin and was gently swishing her hand among the water lilies and the amaryllis. All around her were green, blue, yellow and rust-red ducks, swimming or waddling among the tufts of flowering grass that grew near the water. Ja'far was behind her, motionless, watching. Seeing my master's image in the water, Abassa gave a little scream and turned round. They stared at each other, she on her knees, he towering over her. They did not move, did not speak, but their eyes said everything. Then the princess rose. She was so slim in her embroidered kaftan that she was like the flowers around her. Her hair was braided in a multitude of little plaits adorned with gold threads and pearl and that left her face bare – her face, chiselled like a jewel. She was beautiful: beautiful with her wide black eyes; beautiful with her full and swelling mouth like a child's; beautiful with the bloom of her downy matt skin; beautiful with her teeth; beautiful with her neck and body; and Ja'far was drowning in all this beauty, breathless, without strength before this bottomless well into which he desired to fall.

They took each other's hands for an instant; this act of possession was the only caress they could give each other. Abassa kept her eyes on my master; she was smiling. This man, whose face, whose body and whose power haunted the dreams even of Beduin women of the Arabian desert in their goathair tents, this man was hers; Harun possessed him no longer. He could take his body, but it was of her that Ja'far would be thinking in the embrace, to her that he would be giving himself as he had given himself the night before. Harun had considered her as his chattel, and now she had avenged herself. At the age of fifteen, love is not an island, love is the ocean itself; tumultuous, violent, untamed. Abassa loved Ja'far passionately, with him she had had her first experience of a woman's pleasure, and her jouissance was a source of love. She let herself flow with it, as if she were running water. They stared at each other, and their legs were trembling with the strain of their desire for an impossible embrace.

'May peace be with you, Abassa,' said Ja'far at last. His voice was low and unsteady.

'And with you my lord, peace. To what do I owe the pleasure of your visit?'

'I learned yesterday from the caliph, may God bless him, that you were sick, and I was worried.'

'I was merely indisposed by the heat, my lord, I was burning and my strength had gone out of me. I needed to escape from the sun.'

'There was no sun yesterday, princess Abassa, only the empty sky, for the sun had burnt itself out.'

The servants were standing nearby and were listening; would they repeat their mistress's conversation to the caliph? At last, Ja'far noticed them.

'Abassa, I would like to walk with you in this rose garden, will you?'

Abassa made a sign to her women.

'Follow us,' she ordered, 'we are going to walk in the gardens.' She had not asked them to wait for her. Why? What had she seen, what did she know? This passionate and unreasonable child could also be prudent and perspicacious.

A few steps ahead of me, followed by the two women, they walked through the rose garden. Abassa pointed out the flowers and smelt them. She was laughing, her plaits swaying about her head. Her hands spoke at the same time as her mouth. Ja'far was drinking her in with his eyes, and he smiled at her joy, her words, her gestures. In my heart, I have kept this image like an eternity, a beginning and an end, a ring of beauty and happiness wreathed around that warm and fragrant twilight of the rose garden; and in this perfect, brilliant and polished circle, I look at myself and see my reflection, a cloudy yet precise vision of my face, at one moment a man's, at another a woman's, as if following the light and the days, I was now Ja'far and now Abassa. Beauty and youth, powerful drug, that brings oblivion. We continued to walk in the rose garden; they could not bring themselves to separate. Behind me, the servants were talking, whispering and laughing behind their upraised hands. The palace knew that Abassa was a wife without a husband, and to see this lofty princess punished for a fault they neither knew nor understood both delighted and saddened them – depending on whether the women were speaking of it among themselves or were thinking about it in the solitude of their nights. To have Ja'far al-

Barmaki, the most handsome man in the empire, for a husband, and to sleep alone in one's bed, what a strange and dire fate! For their part, they watched Ja'far but did not dare raise their eyes to his face.

At last, as night was falling, the princess stepped aside.

'I must go in, my lord, I am expected for the evening meal.'

'Will we see you at the caliph's palace? He is anxious that you should visit us.'

'Will you be there?'

'I will.'

'Then I shall see you tonight, my lord, for your presence is for me an imperative summons.'

She turned, took a path between two oleander hedges, and disappeared. I stayed with my master; he remained still for a few instants.

'By God,' said Ja'far, 'how I do thirst for that woman.'

'You shall find refreshment there again, my lord, be sure of it, for the source is as parched as the traveller.'

'I pray that princess Aziza will detain Harun again soon, or else I shall die of thirst!'

He laughed, I knew that he did not for an instant doubt that he would see his wife again.

The days passed. Ja'far and Abassa went on seeing and leaving each other as they had done that day, and their once voluptuous eyes were growing feverish. Each night they waited for a word, a message that never came. Harun called for my master almost every night and, if Ja'far still desired the caliph, he now avoided his caresses when Abassa was there and tried to show an indifference that he did not feel.

Harun, moreover, was careworn. The empire was seized with spasms: there were disturbances in Persia and on the Byzantine frontier, where empress Irene was still paying him tribute. The Alids also preoccupied him, and his aversion towards them made him violent and partial. Ja'far tried to reason with him, to calm him down: men had to be accepted, with all their differences of character and nature. The empire was vast: Muslims, Sunnites, Shiites, Jews, Christians, all races and creeds rubbed shoulders there. People throughout the world admired the liberty enjoyed by each of these communities. He had to pursue this course, show that the Abbasid caliph was the protector of all men, great or small, rich or poor, as God willed it. Harun listened to him but his piety, which was becoming almost fanatical, was driving him to hatred of all that was different from himself. His friend Fadl al-Rabi encouraged him in this direction: the empire had to be purified, purged of the vermin that stank it out; it was God's will. Let them cease with their ridiculous claims and be silent. The caliph approved Fadl al-Rabi's ideas. If it were not for Ja'far, he would have acted. My master knew all this, but his honour forbade him to abandon his friends and he stood up to the situation. When Harun spoke of doing away with the chief Alid, Yahya ben Abd Allah, in Medina, the whole Barmakid clan opposed him, and Harun said nothing. He withdrew his docility into himself like a Greek fire ready to wreak devastation, a force all the more potent for being contained, a violence all the more intense for being hidden. Harun and Ja'far avoided political or religious conversations and began to talk of their past.

Then, one night, an old woman wrapped in a chador came to Ja'far's palace and, in Persian, asked to speak to him. She was led into the hall and a guard came to look for me. I recognised princess Aziza's aunt and took her aside.

'Tell your master to come to my house tonight,' she murmured.

And she went, without another word, without a look.

Ja'far was discussing his affairs with his clients. I went up to him and in a low voice repeated the message I had been given. His face lit up.

'By God,' he said, 'my servant has given me news that delights me and you are all going to benefit from the joy it brings me: go now and do as you please!'

The men rose and dispersed.

'Bring me wine!' he ordered, 'cool wine to celebrate my happiness: we shall drink to the health of princess Aziza.'

While we were drinking, a messenger came to the Golden Palace. The caliph made it known to Ja'far ben Yahya that he would be busy that evening and that he was free to do as he wished with his night. He assured him of his friendship and wished him peace. Ja'far immediately sent the reply that he would be at the palace bright and early the next morning, that he wished the caliph a good and peaceful night. The messenger left and my master burst out laughing. It was as if he were twenty years old again. We set out by the terraces and gardens. The moon was full and lit our way. Women on other terraces watched us and smiled their complicity and indulgence, a mixture of kindly and amused feelings from these women who remembered or hoped. With one bound, we were on the street. We went into the drapers' suq. The house stood in front of us, already familiar and indulgent. The door opened. We entered. The same little servant was smiling in the half light. We did not see the old woman. Ja'far went upstairs immediately and drew back the curtain. Abassa was there, naked, lying stretched out on the bed, and she was staring at him. The heat made her matt body glisten. Her hair was loose, her lips parted, a sweet and violent sensuality emanated from her, an almost animal incitement which fascinated Ja'far so much that he could not move. It was she who called him. He went forward and, still standing, caressed her gently with the tips of his fingers. She closed her eyes.

I lowered the curtain. In spite of the oppressive heat, I felt almost cold. There was a fire burning behind that cloth and its heat was not reaching me. I was filled with a feeling of solitude that I had never known before. I was not Ja'far, he was not me. We were like paired almonds, attached to each other yet separate, different, non-interchangeable. Our difference was Abassa. They were talking to each other, words told like an amber rosary when hands were impatient and the body is febrile: soothing and troubling words, whispered, barely listened to. Their voices blended as their bodies mingled; power of a dream when all solitude seems to have disappeared, when hands grasp, legs entwine and mouth joins with mouth. I had always sought some kind of truth in these moments – a generosity, an exchange, something which made me grow, adding the other to my own measure, making us both a greater, stronger, more fraternal being. Had I found what I desired? I do not know. Old men no longer remember. I have also forgotten how many times Ja'far and Abassa were united at the end of that summer and the beginning of the autumn. Often? Perhaps not, but both of them lived only for those meetings.

Ahmed fell silent. With his head nodding forward, he seemed to be sleeping. The circle around him said nothing and waited attentively. It was drawn out of itself towards the storyteller.

At last, after a few moments of silence, a child asked:

'Is your story finished, Ahmed, for you to be silent thus? Must we come back tomorrow?'

The old beggar raised his head. His gaze seemed lost, as if blind to those around him.

'Tomorrow, yes, tomorrow, if God wills it, for just as the last year of my master's life came to its end in that winter of 186[801–2AD], so, now, is my voice dying out. A year of life was all he could look forward to, and my expectation is no more than a few days. Come back tomorrow, my story will draw to its close and then I will retire to some corner of Baghdad to die: my memory shall be empty, freed of this burden that I have been carrying for so many years, this burden which has been moving inside me and hurting me, for it has become so great.

May each one of you spend the night in peace.

That night, the last night, nobody recognised Ahmed. When darkness fell, he was already in the square, sitting on a little prayer mat of a rare colour and precious design. Where had he obtained this treasure, where had he hidden it? He himself was dressed with great care. He was wearing an embroidered kaftan in faded colours, and a worn black abaya with gold braid, and his grimy turban had been replaced by a kuffiya with an aggal of black wool with silver thread wound about it. His white beard had been combed with great care. He seemed ready for some festivity, an important celebration of which he alone knew the hour. Before the astonished crowd sat an old man who looked like a prince: was his story true then? He really had lived that life of luxury and pleasure! Now, he was surrounded with respect: the people greeted him and the children stepped back in deference. The old man exuded such serenity and such dignity that everyone felt something was about to happen; but what? The end of his story, a farewell perhaps, the beginning of a different life without wandering, without hunger, without poverty. Perhaps he had a house somewhere with servants and a fountain of running water where a family – sons! – were waiting for him! Or perhaps he was going to disappear like an apparition that haunts the moonless nights, a spirit from the past come back among men! He was still and silent, his eyes closed, more dead than alive, waiting to be awakened by the night of memories. The odours of spices, of grilled meats, wafted round the square; a westerly wind was blowing, it was a little cooler. Ahmed opened his eyes.

In December, there was a great feast at the Golden Palace in honour of the chiefs of the Arabian tribes. They served sheep, pigeons in honey, stews with almonds and olives, pastries with semolina and orange flower; no wines, for Harun in his piety refused any fermented drink. There were endless discussions in the Council Chamber; Ja'far was present and so too was Fadl al-Rabi. The empire was growing inflexible and its rigidity made it fragile, ready to crack at any point. Harun no longer accepted either advice or argument: he was withdrawing into himself and, in his entourage, listened only to Ja'far and Fadl al-Rabi, two utterly different men who hated each other. The Syrian advised Harun to divide the empire between his sons. Ja'far disapproved: in his desire that none of them should be wronged, their father was putting them all at a disadvantage. Dismembered, a leopard or an eagle were no more than dead meat, carrion and decomposition. Al-Mamun, his pupil, seemed to my master to be the best qualified to succeed his father; in any case it was he who most clearly resembled him. Fadl al-Rabi was close to Al-Amin, he saw him every day and the adolescent admired him greatly. 'When I am caliph,' he would tell him, 'you shall be my vizier,' and al-Rabi knew that he was telling the truth.

They spoke of the Alid rebellions, of the prisoner of Medina. Ja'far defended him heatedly: it was a matter of honour that they should protect him. Had not Ja'far's brother, Fadl ben Yahya, given him his word? The Barmakids would not just let him waste away: his safety was for them a matter of personal reputation. Harun listened attentively to his friend speak. He said nothing, showed nothing, but, now and again, he exchanged glances with the Syrian, and it seemed that their thoughts were the same.

The Arab chiefs backed Ja'far. They would make no move against the Alid; besides, he wasn't causing them any trouble. As a guest of Arabia, he had their word. They waited for the caliph to give his agreement. He remained with his head bowed under his black kuffiya, his hands on his knees. At last, he raised his eyes and looked around the assembly, stopping at Ja'far.

'Let us consider another subject,' he said.

Ja'far rose and went out.

The whole assembly was plunged into silence. How was Harun going to show his anger? Would this be the end of the Barmakids' arrogance? I had not followed my master; I was watching Harun. He seemed calm, almost amused. On his lips there even formed a strange smile.

Was it chance or concordance of thought? The smile on Fadl al-Rabi's face was the same.

They spoke of other matters. Ja'far was present at the evening meal and sat by the caliph's side. When Harun spoke to him his manner was amicable. The Barmakids could keep their heads high, then. The end of the Arab colloquy was marked by dazzling festivities. Harun presided over them at a distance, surrounded, as protocol dictated, by his two older sons, Al-Amin and Al-Mamun. Beneath the canopy where they were eating the caliph seemed to me careworn, older. His black beard was becoming flecked with silver. He had got heavier. His youth was like a poem that lingers in the memory when the words, already spoken, have merged with the song of the world. Ja'far, only two years younger, had maintained intact the beauty of his body and face. He was like a fruit at the height of summer, soon to be plucked by some sudden gust of wind.

Winter came early and cold. There was some hunting

with falcons, then Harun caught a fever and stayed in
his apartments. In the evening, wrapped in a grey burdah
coat to protect him from the cold wind that blew from
the east, my master went to join Abassa. Stretching out
their arms into the fire of their own bodies, they warmed
their hands with their own ardour.

One morning, Ja'far awoke burning with fever.

'Go to the Golden Palace,' he told me, 'tell the caliph
that my state does not allow me to go to him, that I send
him salvation and peace.'

I went; as the bearer of a message from Ja'far, I was
allowed to enter. I arrived in the caliph's apartments; he
was not there.

As I was about to knock at the door of his private
room, where he sometimes received certain messengers,
I heard his voice and that of the Syrian. There were no
guards, no one distrusted me; I listened.

'I have made my decision, my friend,' said Harun, 'and
it must remain a secret. Send two reliable men to Medina
at once, and have them return immediately to report the
success of their mission.'

Harun stopped for a moment and then went on: his
voice was louder now: 'All this must be done in such a
way as to render groundless any suspicion. The Alids
would make him a martyr, and that is something we
could do without.'

Someone moved. I was afraid that Fadl al-Rabi would
come out and see me. I quickly retreated and hid behind
a hanging. The Syrian did in fact appear. He crossed the
caliph's room and left. I waited a few moments and then
knocked on the door. Muhammad let me in. As I handed
him the missive, I saw Harun at the end of the small
room, sitting by the window reading a message. He did
not raise his eyes to look at me.

However fast it galloped, my horse could not carry

me to my master's palace quickly enough. The crowded suqs slowed me down, the bridge too was blocked. I crossed it, clearing my way with my riding crop. I came into the main courtyard at a gallop. The astonished guards saw me jump from my still-moving horse and dash into Ja'far's apartments. He lay stretched out on his bed under a sable blanket, he was not asleep. Seeing me in such a state, he raised himself on one elbow.

'What is it, Ahmed? You look as if the jinn were after you.'

'Master, in the caliph's apartment I overheard such words that they will make you start up from your couch as a falcon darts from the hunter's fist at the smell of blood. Yahya ben Abd Allah is going to be assassinated, on Harun's orders.'

Ja'far did indeed throw back his blanket and jump up. His features, weary with illness, were now suffused with a boiling anger.

'What did you say, Ahmed, are you sure of this?'

'Certain, master. I heard the caliph's own voice give the order to the Syrian.'

Ja'far quickly threw on a kaftan, his abaya, and wrapped the aggal around his kuffiya. Already, he was at the door.

'Quickly, Ahmed. Let us go to my father's palace: there is not a moment to lose.'

We set off at a gallop. The Ksar al-Tin was not far away, and we were there in a few moments. We had only just dismounted when old Yahya, alerted by the servants that something out of the ordinary was happening, came out of his apartments. Ja'far greeted him, took his arm and led him into the private chamber where the family held its meetings.

'Father,' he said in a voice that was breathless and halting with the effects of the ride and his fatigue, 'father, they are plotting the assassination of Yahya ben Abd Allah.'

'It is not possible.'

'It is the truth, father. We must act immediately.'

There was a long silence as Yahya contemplated his son then, at last, in a calm and tranquil voice, he said:

'My son, I know that you are loath to take sides against the caliph and I understand your reasons. Do you now wish to compromise yourself, perhaps lose yourself in an affair from which you have always wanted to keep your distance?'

'Father, this time it is not a matter of unfounded and endless quarrelling: our honour is at stake and I cannot stand aside. We must act discreetly, get Yahya out of Medina in secret, so that the messengers find his residence empty. The caliph will perhaps not suspect us. Any Alid might be behind such an escape.'

'My son, you are forgetting that Yahya ben Abd Allah will never leave Medina without being forced to do so. He has given his word.'

Ja'far gave a quick laugh.

'The caliph should have no trouble understanding that a promise can be retracted.'

Yahya put his hand on my master's shoulder.

'Are you not acting more against Fadl al-Rabi than on behalf of Yahya ben Abd Allah? Do not allow your decision to be an act of revenge, but an act of honour. The life or death of our friend is of no importance. We are all in God's hands.'

'Father, I know who we are and I know the faith our friends have in us. How could we still retain that faith if they doubted our word: we have never failed to keep it before.'

Behind Yahya, Fadl appeared, accompanied by his son Al-Abbas, who was already a young man.

'Ja'far is right; let us send some trusty servants forthwith and they will persuade ben Abd Allah to go with them. They will bring him here, where no one will dare lift a finger against him.'

Fadl sought my master's eyes and smiled at him.

'You are feverish, my brother,' he said simply, 'go and rest.'

We returned to Ja'far's palace.

The days that followed were filled with anxiety. A game of dice was being played – rapid, inexorable; a man's life was at stake, but was this man really essential? Once more, in my mind, I saw the smiles of the caliph and the Syrian at the conference, and I was afraid. We were gambling for something much more than the simple fate of Yahya ben Abd Allah.

Fifteen days went by; no news came. Ja'far had recovered and saw the caliph every day. Both seemed relaxed, perfectly normal, but both were waiting for a message that refused to come. They spent one night together. What could they say to each other? These two men, set in their determination and their silence, troubled me: what were they trying to prove in their embraces, what were they trying to forget? Was it tenderness, or was it the desire to destroy his lover that led each to match his strength against the other's? Two images: one desired, one rejected. They were no longer giving themselves; instead, each one was drawing from the other the strength he needed for his own self-affirmation. They were like distorting mirrors in which they beheld themselves, finding that they were greater or more powerful than in reality and then being astonished that they could not flow into the twisted forms that had led them astray.

One morning, at dawn, we were awoken by a great bustle in the palace. Two horsemen, exhausted and covered in dust, were asking to see Ja'far, at once. They said that they had come directly from Medina. My master went down at once.

The servants lit the lamps in his chamber. Ja'far dismissed them with one gesture and the two horsemen entered. Shimmering play between the grey of the shadows and light that filtered through the windows and the yellow glow spread by the oil lamps. The flickering of the wicks rippled the silhouettes of the two bowing men, and their shadows on the walls hugged the sinuous contours of the white plaster sculptures. The silence was absolute. Ja'far stood waiting. The two men straightened themselves. One of them stepped forward, and was followed by his shadow, which slid noiselessly over the gold brocade cushions like a silent cat.

'My lord,' he said. 'God is our witness that we obeyed your orders, but your friend was taken from us by a more numerous company. There was nothing we could do.'

I watched Ja'far. Two furrows like bars formed across his brow. His eyes were shining, his voice was cold, imperative.

'How did this happen?'

'We went to Medina, my lord, to Yahya ben Abd Allah's residence. He agreed to follow us only when he learnt that we had orders from the Barmakids. A few hours out of the town, when we were approaching Khaibar, we were overtaken by a company of meharis. There were ten of them – veiled, dressed in black, and armed. We drew our daggers but your friend himself stopped us. "Do not get yourselves killed," he said, "God's will is that I should not leave Medina." He assumed that an Arab chieftain had been informed of his departure and that they would take him back to his residence. A mehara was waiting. He mounted. "My lord," I cried out, "just say the word, and we will fight for you." He turned. "May God give you peace, friends; return to your masters and tell them that they will remain in my memory and in my heart as long as I live." '

'Did he mention our name?' asked Ja'far.

'No, my lord; he spoke of "your masters", that was all.'

'Did anyone follow you?'

'I do not think so.'

'Go,' said Ja'far, 'and do not speak to anyone of what has happened.'

The two men withdrew. I remained alone with my master.

'The caliph was informed of our plan,' murmured Ja'far, 'but by whom?'

'Harun has ears everywhere, master – here in your palace, in the Ksar al-Tin, all around the town and throughout the empire, they overhear even the lowest murmurs.'

'May God protect us!' exclaimed my master. 'The caliph's anger will be terrible. And may He also protect Yahya ben Abd Allah, for his life now weighs no more than a falcon's feather. Perhaps it has already been carried away by the wind of death.'

I tried to restore my master's confidence.

'Perhaps Harun does not know that the men accompanying Yahya ben Abd Allah were of your house. Why should he not suspect Alid partisans?'

'He knows very well where those horsemen were bound. At this very moment, no doubt, spies are reporting this to him at the Golden Palace and, in the morning, be sure of it, the caliph will send for me.'

And indeed, at about ten o'clock, a messenger from Harun's palace came to tell Ja'far that the caliph expected him at once. Ja'far dressed and we left in silence. It was cold. Wrapped in our woollen coats, followed by a few guards, we rode through the town. The streets were quiet; passers-by were hurrying home from the suqs. Merchants were warming themselves around the braziers they had lit in their shops and on the street corners. The grey skies imbued the ochre houses with an earthy colour.

We entered the palace; a dog barked at Ja'far's stallion, making it rear up. My master was almost unsaddled but he did not fall.

This incident was to me a sign of destiny.

The caliph was waiting for Ja'far in his private chamber. He was standing in front of one of the windows. In a corner, Muhammad, his scimitar in his hand, watched us come in; his face was blank.

'May peace be with you!' said Ja'far.

And he stepped forward to kiss Harun's hand. Harun drew back, his eyes angry and cold.

'I accept greetings only from my friends, Ja'far ben Yahya. Are you one such?'

Ja'far's voice did not tremble.

'How could you doubt it, imam? Am I not your brother?'

The caliph stared at him. Ja'far did not move. He seemed calm; he did not lower his gaze.

'My brother, Ja'far! Know that my brothers do not betray me.'

'Betray you, my lord! What do you mean?'

The caliph put his hand on an amber rosary that hung from his belt, but he checked himself and did not take it. His dry voice was growing less assured; he was trembling slightly. Finally, he shouted:

'Then stop defying me, Ja'far al-Barmaki, for I can crush you and can throw you out of this palace like a beggar!'

My master started. Anger was welling up inside him. I feared some irreparable action.

'Master,' I said softly.

Ja'far glanced at me. His anger seemed to wane and he gained control of himself.

'Tell me what I have done to deserve your anger, imam; what have I done to displease you so?'

'Your hypocrisy, Ja'far, astounds me. Can you explain to me how Yahya ben Abd Allah came to leave his residence in Medina?'

Ja'far took a long deep breath. The problem had been posed, clearly and precisely; he could now confront it.

'My lord, I had heard that he was in danger of being assassinated. I knew how much this murder would displease you and the damage it would do to your policy. I wanted to bring him to safety. It appears that he was taken back to Medina, where you will certainly be able to have him protected.'

The caliph was still staring at my master; his anger seemed to be weakening.

'Who spoke to you of an assassination?'

'A rumour, imam, a simple rumour, but I thought it my duty to treat it as significant.'

'Yahya ben Abd Allah will not be assassinated. If he dies now, you will be held responsible for it, for the Arab chiefs no longer trust his word.'

'If it is your will that he live, imam, he shall live, and God shall be with you.'

Harun was becoming relaxed and his long arms were hanging loose at his sides. His stiff posture had eased a little.

'Ja'far, I placed my trust in you and you were not worthy of it. How, after this, will I be able to believe what you tell me?'

Then my master stepped forward and knelt down before the caliph; he took Harun's hand and put it to his lips.

'Harun!'

It was the first time I had heard him call the caliph by his name. His voice was warm, sensual. Harun was quivering.

'Silence,' he ordered. His voice was trembling. 'I have no strength before you and this weakness is most vexatious for me. I never want to hear of Yahya ben Abd Allah again, do you hear, Ja'far?'

Ja'far rose. They were standing face to face, tied together once again by those viscous chains that bound their bodies.

'My trust in you is absolute, imam. I shall fear no more for my friend and I shall never speak of him again.'

The caliph gave a short mocking laugh.

'I have no need to earn your trust, my brother. However I might perhaps solicit your friendship and your desire, and only those things; never forget it! Go now and come back to me at the end of the day. I should like to play a game of chess with you; then we shall sup, and I may desire your company for the night.'

His eyes were glowing as he looked at my master.

'Yes, I may well want you here tonight.'

Ja'far grew pale.

'Imam, I have never failed you or your desire. You do not need to give me orders to make me want to be with you!'

Harun laughed again.

'Do not be angry, my brother, for I assure you that my friendship for you is ardent.'

And, drawing near to Ja'far, he caressed his arm. My master quickly took his hand and clasped it tightly. They looked into each other's eyes. Finally, Harun smiled:

'Go,' he said, 'and come back soon.'

His voice was dull, uncertain, his expression almost imploring. I knew what the caliph was feeling and felt a pang in my heart. We went out.

No one ever knew what became of Yahya ben Abd Allah. He did not return either to his home in Medina or to any other place in the empire. The Barmakids never mentioned him again at court, but they knew, and old Yahya stared in astonishment at Harun, his former ward. Had he then ordered an assassination? A wind of vengeance rose up in Persia, but it was merely a passing breeze: only hurricanes destroy.

In March, the first signs of spring cheered our eyes and warmed our hearts. The almond trees blossomed and, once more, the houses of Baghdad seemed to be exhaling sunlight. Hunting started up again, there were concerts in the gardens, and people rested by the fountains, on the inner patios, where they were out of the wind.

Harun and Ja'far seemed to be at peace. In their looks, their words, their gestures, they were no longer trying to assert a superiority that neither of them really desired. Alone, in the anonymity of some province, these two men would have known true love.

One night, after an intimate dinner, Harun, who seemed to be in fine spirits, let Ja'far go.

'It seems that the spring has brought princess Aziza a new youthfulness. Today, she gave me one of those looks that no husband can resist. I shall go to her tonight. Go, Ja'far, my brother, do not be jealous, for yours is the greater and most noble part of my soul.'

Ja'far bowed. He was thinking that in a few instants he would be with Abassa and his heart was leaping for joy.

The rarity of their meetings had left their desire intact. When they saw each other in the Golden Palace, they were soothed by their confidence and their memories, but when they embraced in the house of the Persian woman, the flame of passion was fanned by the breath of their mouths and grew tall and burnt them. The young girl had become a woman, skilled and passionate; her arms, her legs, her lips took Ja'far just as a liana wraps itself about a tree and he, calm, powerful, gave his strength to this embrace so as to squeeze her even more tightly, to adjust himself to her even more perfectly. United, they were like a murmuring forest, dark, moist, deep; their murmurings were like the stifled cries of hidden beasts; a world, a universe. Sometimes, I would watch them and, like a solitary traveller, I was drawn to them as towards some unlucky country, without frontiers and without a name; and was fascinated and terrified by this secret violence, this implacable egoism.

That night, Abassa, who usually lay naked on the bed waiting for Ja'far, was dressed and standing by the window. She watched us enter; she was wringing her hands. Ja'far stepped forward. She opened her arms and ran to him.

'What is it my sweet?' murmured my master. 'What is the matter?'

With one hand he gently stroked her hair while with the other he held her waist.

Abassa was crying. Her head, resting against my master's breast, was shaken by sobs. He had to take her by the chin to make her look at him.

'Tell me, princess, tell me, what is it?'

Abassa got her breath back and wiped her eyes with the corner of the pink silk scarf that gathered her kaftan at the waist.

'My lord, I do not know what to do. Harun is going to kill me.'

And her weeping began anew.

Ja'far grew worried: he took her by the shoulders and shook her.

'But why, Abassa? Why would the caliph kill you?'

Then, in one breath, the princess, who was still crying, murmured: 'I'm pregnant.'

Ja'far released her and stepped back. How could he have failed to foresee it? How was it that he had not thought of it? He stood there, stunned, not knowing what to say. Abassa was watching him. She was no longer crying.

'What are we going to do?' she asked.

Suddenly, Ja'far's expression changed completely. Throwing his head back, he began to laugh.

'A child! God bless us, I shall have a son from my Abassa!'

The princess stared at him in astonishment, then she too smiled.

'Yes, Ja'far, a gift from God. Nothing could have made me happier, and yet I am going to die.'

'Die, Abassa? Who is going to let you die? You must leave Baghdad, you must go to a quiet place far away from here to give birth to my son. Then, later, you will be able to come back.'

The little princess seemed to have forgotten her sorrow. She was laughing, her hands had taken Ja'far's and their fingers were entwined. Now Abassa's voice was lively, playful.

'I shall go to my maternal grandparents' house in Mecca. They will welcome me and protect me. No one will come to trouble me at their home; not even Harun, who respects and loves me. Soon, I shall announce that I desire to see them again and that I want to spend the summer with them. They are old, my brother will understand my desire to enjoy their tenderness. I shall leave next month; my pregnancy will still be imperceptible then.'

Ja'far put his lips to his wife's hair.

'When will you give birth?'

'In October, if God wills it.' The princess's voice grew sad. 'So many months without seeing you . . . '

'I will go on a pilgrimage to Mecca in the autumn; we shall be together then. Prepare your journey, surround yourself with trustworthy people, all will be well.'

He hugged her and kissed her forehead and her cheeks, and she laughingly gave herself up to his embrace. I did not share their gaiety.

Dawn came. I had not seen the night run by, for I had been deep in thought, my mind wandering over every eventuality, trying to foresee or guess everything that could happen. I was powerless against the danger that threatened my master. I was unable even to define it properly.

On the way back, Ja'far spoke untiringly about his happiness: the family of the Prophet and the Barmakids had founded a line. From now on, the caliph's friendship or disfavour had no power over Ja'far; his child was going to be the cousin of Al-Amin, the son of the haughty Zubaydah, and this thought filled him with a mocking joy. What did it matter that this birth must remain a secret? He would know, and his view of the caliph's family would never be the same again. In Abassa's Hashimite belly, it was the whole of Persia that was developing, growing bigger, preparing to burst out: the whole of Persia, and all those that the Abbasids looked down on from the height of their nobility and purity. My master laughed and his laughter suffocated me.

Some days later, Harun asked Ja'far if he knew of princess Abassa's plan to spend the last days of spring and the summer in Mecca.

'No,' replied my master, 'I never see princess Abassa alone; when I visit her, her entourage of servants prevents any personal conversation.'

The caliph smiled: 'It is well thus, my brother, for that is what I desire, and you know it. Indeed, Abassa's departure is perhaps not unrelated to the fact that she too suffers from the inescapable presence of these people around her. She desires to enjoy a little solitude and rest with her grandparents, may God protect them, and I can understand her. When she returns it would perhaps be best if you stopped going to see her, for this marriage is not making her happy.'

Ja'far gave a short laugh.

'And you talk of a marriage, imam?'

'That is enough,' said Harun, 'perhaps I was wrong to act as I did. My little sister's sorrow is painful to me, for I love her infinitely. We are contemplating a divorce next year and I shall choose for her a husband who, I hope, will make her smile again.'

'I already am her husband, my lord. Do you not want me to make her happy?'

'Not you,' said the caliph drily, 'never.'

Ja'far bowed. I could see the anger rising up in him but he repressed it and a thought I could easily guess even made him smile.

Abassa was preparing her departure. A caravan was ready for the journey: dromedaries for the packs, some saddled meharis, some soldiers from the caliph's guard as an escort. She did not see Ja'far again before leaving, and every night my master waited for a message that never came.

One morning, when we were walking through the gardens on the way to the great ceremonial chamber where some guests were waiting for him, Ja'far said to me: 'Ahmed, I want to give the princess a trustworthy woman who will watch over her and who will be able to give me news of her. I need someone devoted and faithful like Amina. She shall leave with Abassa.'

I started.

'The Afghan, my lord! But she is in love with you, how could she be expected to protect your wife?'

189

Ja'far laughed.

'For the very reason that she is so attached to me: what is mine must be sacred to her.'

'Master, a woman in love is never loyal. I know it.'

Ja'far's laughter became tinged with mockery.

'What do you know of women, Ahmed? Come on, don't give yourself worries for nothing. You see traps and betrayal everywhere, but God is my witness that I can count on my friends.'

That night, after supper, he told me to send for Amina.

Shortly afterwards, the Afghan arrived, veiled. Her eyes were bright and her happiness immediately told me of her mistake concerning the reasons for this summons. She went up to Ja'far and kissed his hand. She was leaning forward, supple, humble and provocative.

'Rise, Amina,' said my master softly, 'I have something to tell you.'

'Yes my lord, I am listening.'

'Amina, you know that my beloved wife, princess Abassa, desires to retire to Mecca to be with her grand-parents . . . '

'I learnt this from the servant woman.'

'I need a faithful and utterly devoted person to accompany her. You shall leave with her. You shall be her companion and the link between her and me.'

Amina started. There was a strange light in her eyes.

'Leave, my lord, leave you?'

'It is my wish, Amina. Take your daughter with you. Princess Abassa will tell you secrets that you must keep locked deep inside yourself. I know that you will do this.'

'I shall do it, master, if you demand it, but it rends my heart to leave your palace.'

Ja'far laughed and I knew that this laugh wounded the young woman.

'I am entrusting my most precious possession into your care.' I trembled at these words. 'What greater proof of confidence could I give you? Go now and be in readiness for the departure.'

Amina stepped back. The light in her eyes was still there.

'Will you keep me with you tonight, master?'

'No,' said Ja'far, 'go back to the other women, I want to be alone. Go!'

He turned away. I wanted to take his arms and put them around Amina. Had he held her then, destiny might perhaps have taken another course. Yes, perhaps it would have done. Those who are loved do not know the thoughts of those who love. I knew them, though, and what I saw in the Afghan's eyes spoke clearly to me. I said nothing: what could I have said? Ja'far's universe was not my own.

One April morning, the caravan which would take the princess to Mecca left Baghdad. She held aside the canopy which hid her, and from high upon her dromedary she looked on her husband for the last time. Their entwining glances seemed unable to extricate themselves, and the swaying of the beast made them seem to be sailing across space on a wave of memories and hopes. A smile separated them, the curtain fell back. Ja'far would never see Abassa's face again. He wanted to escort the princess beyond the town walls on horseback, but Harun held him back.

'Stay,' he ordered, 'I am pained by my sister's departure and I need you here.'

Ja'far gave me the reins of his stallion and followed the caliph. His expression was impenetrable.

The end of April was glorious in the tenderness of its mornings and the sweetness of its nights. We learnt that the princess had arrived in Mecca and had settled at her grandparents' home. That night, Ja'far remained alone. He walked in the gardens and stood a long time at his bedroom window watching the moon. What did he see there? Was he thinking that the same light bathed Abassa's bed, out there in Arabia? That she was resting there, like some tender and palpitating oyster in the nocturnal mother-of-pearl?

'Play me the cithara, Ahmed,' he ordered.

I played, and he stretched out, face down on his bed, and put his head between his arms, and did not move. Finally he turned to face me.

'I should be rejoicing, my friend, and yet I feel sad. The walls of this palace oppress me. If only my body could, like the wind, slip under all those gates to go and find the desert, and melt into its starry nights. Once, my hopes were infinite; I now find myself with only memories and a present which no longer belongs to me. What has happened to me that I should suddenly feel caught in a trap which I never knew had been set? What I have desired, I have had, but I was wrong to give way to desire. Like the soldiers of the Prophet, I should have galloped straight ahead of me to the ends of the earth on a black horse that would carry me and ask of me nothing. Under its hooves, all my desires would have been scattered to the winds, I would have been a match for the world. Ahmed, do you find me handsome?'

'Yes, my lord, you are the most beautiful of men and you know it.'

'That beauty has been my ruin, my friend, it has been a mask hiding my face, making me a magic shadow. I have been desired and have desired no one. I desired only one thing; what? The image of a man, perhaps, that made me dream: at first you, then the caliph. But it wasn't you that I was looking for, it was me.'

I went on playing. Ja'far had closed his eyes.

'Whatever I do now, it will all be petty: the mountain is behind me and I am walking in the plain. What is there for me to do, now?'

I was still playing, a plaintive and nostalgic Persian song.

'My lord, is your desire to be with Abassa so great? Do you miss her as much as that?'

Ja'far looked at me.

'No, Ahmed, I have no need of her, or of anyone. When the caliph has made us divorce, the princess and I, I shall leave Baghdad and never return.'

'Master, Harun will not let you.'

Ja'far smiled.

'Do you believe that, Ahmed, do you think that the caliph is God?'

'My lord, do not say that, those words could do you great damage!'

'I am saying it, Ahmed, and I will do it, I will take my son and we will go to Khurasan or elsewhere. Somewhere, the wheel of my destiny will stop spinning and there we will stay. Not in Baghdad, by God, there is not one face here that I wish to see again.'

He remained silent for a moment and, looking at me, he added:

'Except you, Ahmed, for you are the only one who sees me with my own eyes.'

I stopped playing. We were close to each other, closer than we had ever been. I wanted to touch him, to caress him, but I did nothing. I knew that Ja'far no longer wanted to lend to others the face and the body that they had all loved so dearly. I just said:

'Be in peace, my lord, and think of your son. The obscurity in which he will have to live will make him dependent on your light; do not forget it.'

Ja'far took my hand and clasped it in his own.

'May God protect my son, if I have a son, for he will need such protection.'

I went out and lay down in front of his door. There was no noise from his bedroom.

The only letters Abassa could write were trivial ones and Ja'far was forced to read between the lines. He himself wrote but never gave me a single one of his letters to read. They too had to be banal, for they would be read by Harun's police.

We had a long summer. From May to October, the heat beat down on the town and settled there, making the walls white hot – and likewise the gardens, the ground, even the streets. Ja'far went hunting a great deal. In the evening he came home harassed, soaked in sweat, dusty; then he would take a bath, dine, and join the caliph, or call for one of his concubines. Not one night did he remain alone. In the Golden Palace, Harun organised feasts and dinners where spices inflamed the guests' bodies in the twilight heat. Ja'far shared the caliph's couch and shared his women; and he laughed. I alone knew that his laughter veiled an absence. One night, returning home after a night of pleasure, he told me, as he was lying down to rest:

'Ahmed, I am longing for my child to be born so that a little coolness may enter this palace. Everything rots in these Baghdad summers.'

And, laughing, he added:

'But, by God, how I do love this life!'

He asked for a drink. I brought him a glass of cool water; he downed it in one, wiped his lips and looked at me: 'Ahmed, did you see that young boy who was serving the caliph? He is as beautiful as you were when you were fifteen. Did you see him?'

'Yes, my lord, I did notice him.'

'Do you want me to take him into my service? Harun will not refuse.'

'You are the master, my lord. If you want him, take him.'

Ja'far watched my expression. Seeing that it was impassive, he laughed.

'How serious you are, Ahmed, and how boring. Do not worry, I am going to ask the caliph for him and I shall make him a eunuch for my harem.'

In my mind's eye I saw the face and body of the young boy, and I felt pity for him. Is an unhappy man incapable of spreading anything other than unhappiness?

October's end: soft failing light, soothing the fire of the sky. Grapes, apples and pears were ripe and the children laughed as they ate them in the suqs. In the gardens, banks of flowers bloomed exuberantly and the climbing roses fell in tresses over the barrels where, in the evening, we drank cool wine. Once again, the old folk came out of their houses and the women met on the terraces. Baghdad was emerging from a five-month sleep.

One afternoon, the chief of a caravan from Arabia asked to speak to my master in person.

Ja'far received him. He knew this man would tell him of Abassa.

The camel driver bowed.

'My lord, I come from Mecca and I have a message from your uncle. He asked me to tell you that your servant has given birth to two sons, and that they are in good health.'

Ja'far did not move.

'Thank you for this news and may peace be with you.'

Then he gestured to me.

'Show this man out, Ahmed, and give him his reward.'

The man bowed once more and went out with me. A

few moments later, I returned to my master in his apartments. He was sitting with his head in his hands as if stunned by some shock. I touched his shoulder.

'Two sons, my lord. You see how God is with you.'

Ja'far raised his head. He was smiling, and there were tears in his eyes.

'Ahmed, I feel a happiness that I thought I would never be able to feel again. I must go to Mecca and see my children. I am going to tell the caliph that I wish to go on a pilgrimage.'

'Do not act in haste, my lord. Be patient. If the caliph hears of the camel driver's message, he will be astonished at your eagerness to be with a mere servant woman. For the moment you must do nothing. Wait.'

Ja'far agreed with my opinion. He knew I was right but he was in a great hurry to see his sons. I was sure that he must also be thinking of Abassa.

That evening, there was a feast in the caliph's palace and Ja'far attended but, claiming to be extremely tired, he avoided spending the night there. He returned home to dream of his sons. That day, nothing else could hold his attention.

A full week went by. Then, at the very hour at which the caravan leader had presented himself at Ja'far's palace, a messenger arrived at the Golden Palace and asked to see the caliph in person. He was turned away. The imam was not receiving anyone that day. But the messenger insisted and the guard went to find Muhammad, Harun's slave, who never left him. The tall black man came, listened to the messenger and motioned to him to follow: the caliph received him at once.

In Ja'far's palace, it was an ordinary day. My master received clients, took lunch with his father, walked in the gardens, wrote and talked with his friends. Just as he was making ready to go to the caliph's palace, a messenger arrived carrying a brief letter signed by Harun. 'Do not give yourself the trouble,' said the missive, 'for the feast will not take place. I want to be alone.' There was no greeting and no declaration of friendship. Ja'far raised his eyebrows, folded the parchment and put it in his pocket.

'What do you think, Ahmed?' he asked me.

'Anything is possible, my lord, both the worst or most commonplace of reasons. Tomorrow you will know the wherefore of this message.'

My master did not mention it again. Was he thinking about it? He did not seem worried.

The next day, Ja'far presented himself at the palace. Muhammad, in the reception chamber, prevented him from entering. A guard came to tell him that the caliph was ill. He would not preside over the Council that day. We returned to Ja'far's palace. The day was horribly long. Ja'far tried to throw himself into his activities but could never manage to finish them properly. He ate almost nothing. I knew that he was nervous and worried. Evening came; there was still no message from the Golden Palace. Ja'far had written the caliph a note asking for news. He had received no reply. That night he could not sleep. Did Harun know something? Were Abassa and her sons in danger? At dawn, pale, his cheeks prickly with stubble, and with dark rings around his eyes, he decided to go to the caliph's palace, to see him, whatever the cost, and to find out the reason for his silence. We arrived in the early morning. Muhammad straight away led us to his master. Harun was standing in front of the basin on his patio. He was reading a poem. He smiled when he saw us enter.

'May peace be with you, Ja'far. To what do I owe the pleasure of your visit so early in the morning?'

Ja'far kissed Harun's hand.

'Imam, I was worried about you. Your silence made me fear that you were sick.'

'I am in fine form my friend, as you see. I am even reading a few lines on the vanity of worldly things, on their deceitful beauty. Do you love life, Ja'far?'

'My lord, you know very well that I do.'

'You are right. Life is a gift from God. Read, read this poem then, it is most beautiful, and let us walk together.'

Ja'far grew less tense. I could see his features relaxing, his hands opening. He smiled at me but I did not return that smile. Something indefinable oppressed me: perhaps Harun's expression or his voice, something abnormal about his behaviour that frightened me. I wanted to talk to my master but I could not. He had spent hours worrying, why force him to relive them? I had only my intuition to go by.

The next day, old Yahya came to his son's residence. He came to announce his imminent departure on the pilgrimage to Mecca. The night before, the caliph had told him that he wished to travel there in his company, and with his sons Al-Amin and al-Mamun. Why this sudden decision? He did not know. He must begin to prepare now, and had come to bid farewell to his sons. Ja'far grew pale.

'Does the caliph wish me to go with him?'

'He did not mention it,' replied Yahya. 'I was only informed of his decision by a messenger.'

When his father had left, my master remained paralysed with worry. Harun in Mecca! What was the real purpose of this journey? He went to the Golden Palace. The caliph gave him his customary welcome. He left it to Ja'far to bring up the subject of the forthcoming pilgrimage.

'Do you want me to go with you, imam? I would rejoice to be at your side.'

'No, Ja'far. I want to be sure that you are here in Baghdad. You shall take the reins of government. You are the only person I trust.'

My master bowed.

'When are you leaving, my lord?'

'Tomorrow, my friend, if God wills it. The princes shall go with me. You shall have only political responsibilities and I know that you will serve me well. Go now, I have much to do tonight and I will see you when we leave. I shall expect you at the end of the morning; may God protect you.'

When we arrived in the Golden Palace the next day, a chamberlain came to tell us that the caliph had brought forward the hour of his departure and that the caravan was already far away; they had left Baghdad at dawn.

Long, slow days and nights. In mid-November we heard that they were in Mecca. No message; silence, a silence that cast morosity over our amusements, that made our food and drink bitter. An east wind was blowing, harbinger of an early winter. Olives were cool and dates melted in the mouth. A whole world was disappearing and would reappear only in spring. Ja'far would never see the fine days again.

It was then that my master started to spend a lot of time with his brother Fadl. Together, they would talk of the affairs of government, from which Fadl had long been barred. They would exchange points of view and share the same emotions. In the evening of their lives, the two brothers found each other as they had been in childhood: profoundly united. Contact with Fadl made Ja'far more resolute; he banished his fears and anxieties; was he not a Barmakid, why then should he tremble like a scolded servant? Finally, they began to speak of the caliph. Harun's name had never been mentioned before. Ja'far knew that his brother condemned the bonds that tied him to Harun; he had never tried to justify himself. Henceforth, as if they knew that their personal feelings were of no importance now, they no longer avoided speaking of themselves. Fadl listened to Ja'far and Ja'far listened to Fadl; they understood each other and knew that they were alone against the caliph. Harun was trying to escape from them so as not to be smothered by their friendship, their tenderness, their love, so as no longer to feel that they cast a shadow over his power, so that he would no longer have to acknowledge their intelligence, their strength, their superiority. He hated them all now and did not dare show it, Fadl was sure of that. As for Ja'far, he knew that the caliph still desired him, that he had only to touch Harun for his eyes to darken with desire and his breath to come quick and short. Yes, he still had a real power over Harun, but he no longer wished to use it. He was tired of that game; it left him only disgust and bitterness now. And yet he loved Harun, they had shared too many moments of their lives for them not to be a part of each other. God was his witness that on the slightest sign from the caliph he would come running. Harun had loved him, too, but he detested that love.

In the late afternoon, when the flies seemed gilded as they danced in the rays of the setting sun, the two brothers would walk in Ja'far's gardens. Often they fell silent; they had said so much that words no longer mattered. My master had told Fadl of his contempt for Harun's orders, and of the birth of the twins. Fadl had given his brother a long look:

'The gulf into which we are about to fall has been there for all eternity. Our lives have taken their course, but it is said that some men, unable to leave their path, forget their eyes and their ears and follow only their hopes. We are such men. Servants with the souls of masters are banished from all residences, for it pleases the weakness of the lords to stand alone like the eagle on the mountain, even though they are shivering with cold and fear. Our sons will hold their heads high when they think of us, for they shall know that we never bowed our own in submission.'

Fadl was silent for a few moments and took his brother by the shoulders.

'Ja'far, God gave you many gifts and you have scattered them in every wind. In the spring, shoots will appear, rooted in you; together, those shoots will form a sheaf. The ambition we all cherished was not to win, it was simply to progress. Our father taught us to accept the thoughts and actions of others without expecting results. May God bless him, for he has given us a liberty that none can take away.'

Early in that month of December, the sky was extraordinarily luminous. The rays of the full moon swept the thousands of stars into bouquets. I wished I was a jinni harvesting those shining beams, gathering them into sparkling sprays that would shed light on my fears.

The caliph was on his way back. In mid-December, horsemen announced the imminent arrival of the pilgrims. They were already in Iraq, near El-Hammam. Ja'far wanted to go to meet them. Fadl dissuaded him.

'If the caliph knows nothing, then leave him the time and the space to desire you. If he knows the truth, then do not anger him further.'

Three days went by, then the advance guard of the escort arrived before the walls, carrying black flags. Behind them came a caravan, moving forward in a cloud of dust. Two horsemen were riding side by side, surrounded by soldiers: Yahya and Harun. The caliph was dressed in black, his old tutor in white. They were not talking to each other. Above them, swept by the easterly wind, the sky was indigo blue. A light yellow dust flew around the hooves of the horses and the meharis. We could not distinguish the faces of the horsemen yet, only their silhouettes were visible: the cloth of the kaftans billowing in the wind, their turbans or their kuffiyas. The banners flapped, the troops were silent. The people of Baghdad had gathered on the ramparts. The women's trills of joy rang out, the children jostled each other and the guards assembled on either side of the Kufa gate, preventing anyone from approaching. Preceded by Muhammad and two soldiers carrying standards, who were followed by the princes, Harun and Yahya entered Baghdad to the joyous clamour of the crowd. Ja'far stood in his private chamber, waiting. He had hesitated before going to the Ksar al-Tin and had eventually given up the idea. Now all he could do was be still, live in the midst of what he loved; his home, last earth, last refuge for the weary traveller he had become.

The caliph did not send for him that same day, but only the day after; even then, his gaiety was forced, his laughter ironic and hard. He hugged Ja'far and took a long look at him.

'It is good to come back to one's friends,' he said, 'for I have few enough in my entourage.'

'Did the pilgrimage go as you wished, my lord?'

'Reality does not always grant me my wishes, Ja'far. Now I accept what God is pleased to send me. Dreams are childish toys. By thought and prayer, I have at least come to understand that. Did you think of me?'

'Every moment, imam, for my life is but the shadow of your own.'

Harun smiled.

'Shadows are sometimes strange and threatening, Ja'far, sometimes familiar, too; it all depends on the light. Come, Ja'far my friend, let us not philosophise, I want to see you at my side, I want to look at you and hear you talk, for God sometimes takes back what he has given. One day, perhaps, you will no longer be with me.'

He said this with an almost tender smile on his face, and he looked at Ja'far as one considers some marvellous and fragile object.

The last chrysanthemums were dying now and their golden petals floated on the blue basin, derisory craft painted in the colours of regret. A few bees still hovered among the climbing vines, around the sun-dried grapes. Sweetness of departure, sweetness of sleep, the heat slid across the green faience of the mosaics, imparting a sparkle to the eyes of the nymphs and dolphins that embraced there, figures forever frozen in the same ordered and lifeless decors that the sun and the nights in the caliph's garden had beheld now for so many years.

Together, Harun and Ja'far studied the affairs of the empire. The caliph insisted on understanding and knowing everything, as if he wanted to read to the very last line of a book he was about to close for ever.

One night, at the end of December, Ja'far was preparing to leave when Harun detained him. Since the return of the pilgrims, they had not spent a single night together.

'My brother, I would like you to organise a falcon hunt in a few days' time. I would be happy once more to share this pleasure as we have done so often before. Will you do this?'

'I desire only to obey you, imam, and it will be my greatest joy to hunt with you.'

Harun laughed. He was looking at Ja'far as one looks at a child.

'In three days' time?'

'Everything will be ready, my lord. We shall leave at dawn.'

The caliph put his hand on my master's arm.

'Since we shall have to leave early, Ja'far, we shall not separate. I have not had your company for a very long time, and I miss your warmth. You shall stay with me the night before and we will try once again to taste the intoxication that made me so weak I could no longer hold up my head. Your power, Ja'far, is so dangerous that it seems inoffensive and one exposes oneself to it unarmed. I shall face that danger once again, for I cannot forget the caress of your skin, of your mouth, your hands. Today, I shall take that gift; God alone disposes of the morrow.'

Ja'far and Harun did not see each other until the eve of the hunt. My master had given orders that falcons, horses and servants should be ready at dawn the next day. Ja'far was calm, peaceful, but he seemed to have lost all joy in life. He was thinking of his sons. Did his intuition tell him that he would never see them?

On that last night, as Harun had asked, they stayed together. Precious perfumes burned in the caliph's chamber. The bed had been covered with furs and silk cushions. The darkness was almost total, a temple for the celebration of some secret ceremony or ultimate sacrifice. Yellow flowers bloomed in amber ceramic vases and, in the silk-curtained windows stood jade cups overflowing with black grapes, purple figs and ochre-coloured dates. Harun was wearing a gold brocade kaftan and stood waiting for Ja'far in front of a lamp that had been placed on the floor, and which projected his shadow on to the wall like a Chinese lantern. He watched him enter, and, for the first time since his return, I saw affection in his eyes. Ja'far stopped several paces away from him. The flickering light caressed them both with its blonde breath, and the smouldering perfumes wreathed themselves around the silks and furs, licked their skin and their hair like a courtesan drunk with love. The two men observed each other and in their eyes appeared a whole world of memories, sensations and affection.

My master stepped forward.

'How beautiful you are, Ja'far!' murmured the caliph. 'I had forgotten that beauty.'

Then, without taking his eyes off Harun, Ja'far unfastened his belt and unbuttoned his kaftan, which fell to his feet; he stood naked before the caliph who, drawing closer to him, caressed Ja'far's shoulders with the tips of his fingers, caressed his chest, his belly – as if he dared do no more. Ja'far opened his arms; his eyes were bright, his breath came short and quick; a first coming together, a last offering, a love affair somewhere between a handful of fleeting instants and the span of a whole life. The lamp light was flickering, and Harun was trembling with desire, trembling with his memories and with the becoming of daily life. What would happen to his memory? How would he bear it from now on when, seeking refuge there from the present, he found that this memory brought him only the image of Ja'far's body, his arms open wide, when he found Ja'far's eyes and mouth, and his own desire for that skin, that odour and that warmth, now dissolved in the river of past time?

The caliph closed his eyes and the hours became stars scattered through the sky of their night.

At dawn, Muhammad came to inform his master that the hunt was ready to set off. Neither Harun nor Ja'far had slept. Together, without speaking, they shared their fruit and sour milk. More than their mouths, it was their eyes that remembered.

It was a brisk early morning and the horses set off at a gallop. Ja'far and the caliph rode at the head; the falconers followed with their hooded birds on perches fixed to their saddles; we were going north of Baghdad, two hours out of the town, to a bare plain where game could not escape the predators.

Wrapped in his woollen burdah, the caliph was silent. Beside him, Ja'far's gaze fell elsewhere; their bodies brushed together and recognised each other; but now their respective paths were forking apart even more quickly than their stallions could gallop. The love of the caliph and the vizier was now only a reflection, an echo, an image.

A hare, a grouse, a bustard were killed; wrought to a frenzy by the blood, the falcons beat their wings and hopped with impatience on their perches. The sun was at its zenith. They were hoping for a young gazelle, but it did not appear. A pigeon took to flight and the caliph had his falcon released. The bird, moving in wide circles, waited for its prey; its light, aerial flight easily encompassed the clumsy and heavy movements of its victim, which was trying to alight. In a flash, the predator was upon the pigeon, blood spurted forth; with one bound, the falconer was beside the bird and had called him back. Docile, the falcon settled on his fist and was given a strip of raw meat, which it tore from its master's hand. The servant bent down and picked up the pigeon and offered it to the caliph. Harun took it. The bird was still heaving with spasms. Then, as if he had touched some horrific object, the caliph threw it to the ground and a ghastly pallor came over his face. He wiped his hand on his coat and a red stain bloomed like a faded rose petal; yes, like a rose petal or the mark of a wound.

The hunters returned; the hunt had been poor. They had to arrive before the supper given by the caliph for his intimate friends. All the most powerful and the most noble men in the empire were there, and all of them saw Ja'far take his seat at Harun's side. Immobility of ritual; only the caliph's attitude had changed. He wanted to stand alone; he was the master. He looked neither to Ja'far nor to any other man; there was an insulating, protective wall erected about him. Harun had now become an image, his own. My master watched the caliph in silence. Little by little, Harun was drawing in the thread of their tenderness. When would he cut it? A few days earlier Ja'far had thought of leaving Baghdad, but such a departure would have looked too much like flight, a flight from silence and absence, not from any danger. If Harun had thrown back in his face what he had discovered in Mecca, then perhaps he would have been able to get round the problem, perhaps he would have managed to defuse the caliph's anger. But this cold tenderness, this mute friendship had chilled him, and it had become impossible now to make a gesture. Ja'far, who so loved to play, held in his hand pieces that he no longer knew how to move; his silent adversary observed him with a smile and his hands wandered, not knowing where to go, what to take, where to settle. Then the caliph seized the board and, with a great laugh, scattered the pieces. Ja'far had not lost, he simply had not been able to play.

While the servants were bringing the ragouts, Harun leant towards my master.

'You are hardly eating. Are you unwell?'

'I am tired, my lord, the night was short and the hunt long.'

'You are going to rest, Ja'far, yes, you are going to rest, and your fatigue will leave you. Me, I have no desire to sleep tonight, and my weariness will remain. You shall sleep and I shall watch. No doubt, luck is on your side.'

'Do you want me to stay with you, my lord?'

'No, my brother, my fatigue is so great that I want to be alone. The presence of a friend, however sweet, is not eternal, and I must learn the way of solitude.'

Ja'far said nothing. He was not afraid; perhaps he felt some anguish, some obscure presentiment, but nothing more. When the herb-roast sheep arrived, the caliph called for the eye and gave it to my master.

'You deserve it, my friend, for everything about you.'

All eyes were on Ja'far and Harun. Their love seemed to be without end. The two men exchanged looks, but the caliph no longer saw my master.

At the end of the meal, Harun rose and, addressing his guests, said: 'I am going to leave you, my friends. Finish this meal without me, for I am weary and am going to rest.'

Ja'far also rose.

'Stay, Ja'far. Enjoy this feast which I have given for you!'

For a few seconds, his eyes settled on my master, on his face, his mouth, his shoulders . . . then, abruptly, he turned and strode boldly out of the banqueting hall. The curtain masking the door fell back behind him.

My master stayed only a few moments more, then returned to his palace. The night was clear, studded with stars, peaceful. We walked to our horses; it was not cold. A few dogs barked. The streets smelt of mandarins, spices and leather. Two men passing by greeted us and we returned their greeting.

In front of his palace, Ja'far reined in his horse and looked up at the sky.

'I shall have to learn astrology,' he murmured, 'for these immensities fascinate me and make me melancholy.'

'Do you have cause to grieve, my lord?'

'Perhaps, Ahmed, or perhaps not. Are not the Persians a sad people?'

'That is true, master, but are we still Persians?'

'What are we then, Ahmed, if we are no longer Persians?' We entered the main courtyard. The guards hurried up to take our horses. Ja'far walked slowly back to his apartments. He stopped at the edge of the basin, took some water in his hand and drank, then, taking one last look at the sky, he went inside. I helped him to undress. I brought him a vermeil bowl and some fine linen for him to wash his face and hands. He smiled at me.

'I long to see my sons. I do not even know their names.'

'You shall see them, my lord. Princess Abassa must be languishing for you!'

'Will she be able to wait for me? She is young, passionate, and I am so far away!'

'She will wait for you, for she loves you and you know it.'

Again, Ja'far smiled.

'Do you really believe she loves me? She loves the man the caliph loved, the man Harun refused to give her. It is my sons that she will really love.' He was silent for a moment then added: 'As we shall both love them, God willing.'

He wiped his hands with care and slipped on a fine white cotton galabiya.

'I must sleep Ahmed, I am most weary tonight.'

'May God protect you, my lord. I shall stay in front of your door and watch over you.'

Ja'far put his hand on my shoulder.

'Are you then my only friend, Ahmed? I wish you a night of peace.'

I closed his chamber door and lay down in front of it. A little later, hearing no noise, I entered, silently: lying on his belly with one arm hanging down from his couch, Ja'far was sleeping. He seemed calm, at peace. I retired.

What time was it when the caliph's guards arrived? It was well before dawn. No cock had crowed. I jumped to my feet. They shoved past me and pushed open my master's door. Ja'far awoke and rose up as soon as he saw them come in. I was still trying to keep them back but they drew their scimitars and kicked with their boots. Ja'far was on his feet now, groping for his dagger. Two men grabbed hold of him. He struggled and managed to break free.

'Do not touch me, dogs, your mange defiles me!'

Two other guards took his arms and twisted them behind his back, trying to force him to his knees, but Ja'far's strength prevented them.

'Help!' cried my master. 'Ahmed, my guard!'

One of the soldiers began to laugh:

'You no longer have a guard, Ja'far al-Barmaki. The caliph has decided it. You have nothing now and you are going to die.'

With a prodigious effort, my master broke free.

'Are your orders from the caliph? Dispatch then, but quickly!'

And, turning to me, he cried:

'Go, Ahmed, for the love of God, and for my sake!'

I refused.

'I shall never leave you, master, I shall die with you.'

Then a soldier struck me on the face with the flat of his scimitar, and I fell back. He laughed:

'You are about to see the death of your master, dog! Watch carefully!'

Ja'far was no longer trying to defend himself. Two men forced him to his knees: a third, coming from behind, made a gaping wound in Ja'far's neck with a great blow from his scimitar. Blood gushed on to the silk carpet where wreaths of blue flowers and roses wound about firebirds; their blood-bespattered colours were even brighter now. Ja'far fell forward. A second blow from the scimitar severed his head. I retched.

Then, trampling over my body, the soldiers left, carrying my master's head by the hair. A pool of blood spread out around his corpse. I crawled up to him. My ribs were shattered. I plunged my hands into the red liquid that was escaping from the shoulders and spread it over my face. I could still feel his warmth, the sweat on his body . . . Then . . . I can't remember clearly . . . a woman told me to leave, that all the servants must disperse; and I went. Where? My memory cannot tell me.

One night, I woke up shouting in an unknown bed. An old man approached with a lamp in his hand. He spoke Arabic with a Persian accent. He was a friend. He had found me in the street, doubled up with pain, absent, and had brought me to his house. I learnt that my master's head had been spiked on one of the bridges of Baghdad and that the onlookers were milling past to see what remained of his pride and his beauty. I learnt that Yahya and Fadl had been arrested that same night and taken far from Baghdad, to Raqqa, to a citadel that none ever left. The palace of the Barmakids was the caliph's property now. The servants had left. Silence now dwelt within those walls. In the gardens, the flowers were wilting; the birds were dying in the aviaries. Strange presences still wandered there, warding off the caliph's guards at dawn and at twilight.

I recovered, but inside me there were two strong hands that were pulling me down into a deep hole, lower and lower, faster and faster. From the bottom of this pit, I looked up at the sky, but it was now so far away that it had lost all its brilliance. In order to rebuild myself, to climb out of that ditch, I had to find the scattered fragments of my being, to put them together; I had to leave for Raqqa, then for Mecca.

Ahmed fell silent. The expression of this noble old man in his frayed kaftan was blank now: his eyes were stagnant water in which a whole life was reflected. No tears; indifference to the present, desertion of the man he now was – the solitary and strange old creature he had never inhabited. On the great square of Baghdad, he fell silent, and the men and women standing around him fell silent also; their minds were turned towards another time and place that were rising out of the night, they were the slaves of an old man who could wind them in and reel them out to the rhythm of his memory. It was hot, it was late, but time was suspended like a falcon hovering in the breeze; immobile, light, immaterial, eternal. Ahmed looked up at the stars.

The night is unfolding and at dawn I wish my spirit to be in peace. Go or stay, soon there will be no storyteller, there will only be an old man facing death.

I left for Raqqa on the Persian's mule. I had to see Yahya and Fadl; they must know in their solitude that their servants had not forgotten them. It was bitterly cold when I arrived in the town that I had once known bustling with the pleasures of the court. How would I manage to see my masters? I did not know, but with God's help I would succeed. I knew some guards and servants at the palace, and in particular there was a groom who spoke to me often and whose eyes barely concealed the attraction he felt for me. I saw him, he recognised me and was afraid, for the name of the Barmakids made them all tremble. I reassured him. I was not dangerous. I just wanted to see them. He asked me what I would give him if he helped me. I smiled and took his hand. He understood: yes, he would help me.

Every day, escorted by guards, Yahya and his son took

a walk in the inner courtyard of the citadel. Sometimes, servants came by on their way to the kitchens or the gardens. He could take me with him. We would be carrying bundles of firewood in our hands and would be heading for the guard room to rekindle the fires in the braziers. With the cold, the comings and goings of the servants were incessant.

Behind the door of the woodshed, we waited to see the prisoners. Time passed. The groom sometimes took my hand but I withdrew it abruptly. White light of winter in the paved courtyard. The breath of the guards dissolved into it; their steps echoed loudly on the marble flagstones.

At last, Yahya and Fadl appeared, escorted by some soldiers. At first I did not recognise them. They were shrouded in woollen coats like those of shepherds and their feet were bare in their leather sandals. Yahya was now a frail and bent old man like a tree bowed by the east wind. Fadl was supporting him on his arm. He had grown thin and was pale, but he still had the same proud expression. In his eyes, I rediscovered the eyes of my master, and the shock – violent as if from a fist – made my breast shake.

Side by side, we came out of the shed and forward into the courtyard. Neither the prisoners nor the guards saw us. I approached. A guard glanced at me, saw the wood and looked away. He even stepped aside to let me pass. I pretended to stumble and the wood fell out of my hands. I swore loudly. At the sound of my voice, the Barmakids turned towards me. Fadl was the first to recognise me. He took his father's arm and uttered a few quick words in Persian: 'Our servant.' The old man looked at me. There was joy in his eyes at this new glimpse of a world he thought had disappeared. Then was it the cold wind blowing, or his memories, that brought the tears to his eyes? How could I speak to them, how tell them that they were not alone, that even here, distant prisoners, the woof of their people's affection was woven around them for ever? Father and son had stopped in their walk and were watching me pick up the wood. What were they hoping for? A moment of my life was all I could give them. Fadl was the first to speak.

'You have a heavy load, my friend, have you no one to help you?' I pointed to the groom, who was standing watching me, wide-eyed with panic.

'There are two of us, my lord, but it is so cold that we are constantly having to rekindle the fires.'

'It is indeed cold. The winter seems endless. Will we ever see the spring again?'

'Certainly, my lord, we shall see it again soon.'

A guard came up.

'Get along there, don't linger. It is forbidden to talk to prisoners.'

I finished picking up the wood and looked at them for the last time.

'May the peace of God be with you!'

'Are you staying in Raqqa, my friend?'

'No, my lord, I am going to set off on the pilgrimage to Mecca.' Yahya nodded. He had understood.

'May God protect you on your pilgrimage, my friend, and may he give you peace.'

The guard took my arm and forced me aside.

'I told you not to talk to the prisoners. Go, or you shall be whipped.'

I followed the groom, who had already made off. One last time, I turned back. I saw the Barmakids, thin and meagrely clothed, standing in the wind of that glacial winter. What was left of the caliph's superb viziers? Two men holding on to each other so as not to fall.

I would never see either of them again. Yahya was the

first to die, two years later; Fadl went three years after his father. I heard in the meantime that he had been atrociously beaten for trying to make contact with a friend. He was left for dead. He had lived on for many months more. One evening, when he had just finished his prayer, Harun was told of his death. His piety had become fanatical now, and the austere figure of Fadl al-Rabi was always at his shoulder. He read the message telling him that his foster brother was no more: after Ja'far, after Yahya, he was the last of the great Barmakids. The letter fell to Harun's feet, he raised his hands to his face and murmured: 'I shall not survive them.' The caliph died a few months later. I heard these words from a servant who had been by his side and whose wife was a Persian.

I now had to go to Medina to see Abassa and my master's children, to be by their side as I had been by their father's. I had no other reason for living, no other reason for hoping. When a caravan carrying spices and silks was about to leave Baghdad for Arabia, I asked to serve the caravaneers and look after the camels. I was accepted. The road was long and hard. The mild Iraq spring was already hot on the edges of the desert. During the cold nights, I lay down in the warmth of the beasts. I looked up at the sky and tried to understand the will of God. Sometimes, the features of Ja'far's face eluded me. I saw his eyes, his nose, his mouth, but each part was separated from the whole as if it had shattered into a thousand pieces in my memory, a red rose plucked by the winter wind, petals scattered on a silk rug with a pattern of red flowers, like spots of blood. Sometimes, I heard his voice in my sleep: 'Are you then my only friend, Ahmed?', or 'Go, Ahmed, run, for the love of God, and for my sake!' Then I would rise up with sweat pouring down my face, biting into my lips so as not to cry out. The camel drivers looked at me and nodded. They felt neither curiosity nor contempt for the insane, only pity.

The caravan stopped for a few days at Medina. I slept on street corners and earnt my food by helping craftsmen in the suqs. I had no possessions now, only this rug that you see before you and the kaftan I am wearing, which belonged to my master: a palace servant had given them to me.

Smaller now, the caravan set off again. I was servant to an old merchant who liked to tell me the story of his life. The camels walked slowly; play of shadows and light on the desert sand to the swaying rhythm of their silent, supple steps. The men slept, rocked by this moving and regular wave that rippled under the burning sun. The water was cool in our mouths and on our parched lips. From time to time, rising up on the horizon, silent, abandoned, gardens and patios came before my eyes. The fountains were no longer flowing, the mosaics were covered with moss. Where did they come from, these lawns, these basins, these edifices rising out of the desert? Why did they resemble Ja'far's palace? I closed my eyes, but no doubt they were inside me, for they were still there; unmoving, clear as a summons.

At last, nestling amid the grey hills, like a stone in the palm of God's hand, we saw Mecca, the goal of my journey. I stood there for a long time, contemplating the walls of the town, brown belt around Ja'far's children. At last I would be able to kneel before them!

Unfamiliar streets. I had been on a pilgrimage to the Holy City only twice. The houses were all alike, their doors closed. The residence of Abassa's grandparents was the most imposing in the town: high walls pierced with windows sheltering behind cedarwood mashrabiyahs;

ochre and white façade between two square towers, wooden doors with bronze studs. I knocked hard. Behind a judas, someone was watching me; a voice asked:

'What do you want, stranger?'

'I have come from Baghdad to see princess Abassa.'

'Princess Abassa does not receive visitors. Who are you?' The voice was dry, sharp.

By God, I knew that man would open the gate at once when he heard my name.

'I am Ahmed, the servant of Ja'far ben Yahya al-Barmaki.'

There was a silence.

'Do not move, stranger. I am going to speak to the master.'

I waited for a few moments and then the door opened. There, lit by a soft light from the patio, an old man in a white kaftan was standing in the hallway. He was observing me and his expression was both kindly and anxious at the same time.

'Are you really from the house of the Barmakids, stranger?'

'I am. Princess Abassa will recognise me.'

'Then may God's peace be with you. My home is yours. Follow me.' I penetrated with him into the patio with its floor of round pebbles. A marble basin babbled at its centre and there was an old fig tree against the wall. It was a warm, comfortable place. For the first time since the death of my master, I felt a kind of peace. On the other side of the patio there opened a great salon, then a small room furnished with cushions, rugs and a few low tables in carved wood. The old man stopped there. I bowed before him and kissed his hand. With one movement, he bid me rise.

'Have you come from Baghdad to see my grand-daughter?'

'For the princess and her children, my lord, the sons of my master, his last joy.'

Imperceptibly, the old man's features grew tense, but he still looked upon me with kindness.

'Did you not know, my friend, that the twins were taken away from my granddaughter?'

I was struck dumb by this news, but my expression must have answered him, for the princess's grandfather quickly gave me a seat. My mind tried desperately to find something to hold on to, but it could not. All I could see clearly was the bronze bird with a crown that was standing on the table in front of me. I noticed that its beak was open and there was a handle on its back. It was probably a ewer for washing one's hands. The old man respected my silence for a few instants.

'One night, even before we had heard of Ja'far's death, some men came. They forced open the door of my home, pushed past my servants and then myself who, alerted by the shouting, had come down to meet them. The two children were sleeping in the nurse's room. They seized them and, when the woman held one of the abductors back by his coat, he cut off her hand.

'The princess saw them run off with her babies. I took her in my arms. There was nothing we could do. We have never found out what happened to them. I have searched and asked questions. I asked all the chiefs of Arabia if they could tell me something about this infamy; no one knew anything. My friend, I desire no more than God's will, but the princess, who heard of her husband's death a few days later, is a broken woman. She looks sixteen, it is true, but her heart and her spirit are dead. Do you still want to see her?'

'Yes, my lord, for princess Abassa was dear to my master and I am her servant.'

My host clapped and a young girl came running up.

'Ayisha, go and tell the princess that a cousin has come to visit her from Baghdad. She may receive him in her apartments.'

I was given a glass of cold water and some dates. A little serving girl glided noiselessly on the terracotta slabs; a woman walked past with a basket overflowing with vegetables perched on her head. This vast residence was astonishingly silent. No children played there, no one spoke. From the small windows there fell a weak, pale light which left whole corners of the rooms I had been through in shadow. A cat jumped nimbly on to one of the cedarwood tables and sat there observing me. The only noise was the buzzing of the flies as they darted about in the rays of sunlight.

Finally, the young girl returned. I had not heard her, and so I jumped.

'The mistress is waiting for you, my lord.'

The old man showed me the way. I followed him through vast rooms. We crossed another patio. At the end, a sculpted wooden door stood ajar. My host knocked and we entered.

Abassa was sitting on a low seat in front of the window. Through the mashrabiyah, the sun traced triangles of light and shadow. Her head was turned towards the street. All I could see was the mass of her curly hair and the back of a white satin kaftan. She did not seem to hear us and made no movement towards us. Her grandfather went nearer.

'Abassa,' he called in a gentle voice.

The princess did not start, but turned her head slowly towards us. She looked at her grandfather first, then her eyes fell on me and her smile froze.

'Ahmed!' was all she said. And, with that, she turned her head back towards the streets. Her grandfather touched her shoulder.

'Abassa, Ahmed has come from Baghdad to see you.'

The sun made auburn highlights in the princess's hair. On the window ledge, just in front of her, stood a pink marble cup full of almonds and dried black grapes. From the street below could be heard an occasional call, or the sound of footsteps or wheels. The cat had followed us. He jumped on to the princess's knees. She did not touch him. In the half light, I saw the profile of my host and his sad smile.

Abassa again turned to look at us. With one hand she was stroking the grey cat's back. She smiled at me.

'I am happy to see you again, Ahmed. What news do you bring? Have you seen Ja'far? Did he not have anything to say to me?'

I had no idea what to reply. The old man put his hand on my arm.

'Don't worry, Abassa. Everything is all right. Ahmed has simply come to give you his greetings.' We looked at each other. There was no sadness in the princess's brown-green eyes. All they saw was a sequence of vague and sweet thoughts. She began to stroke the cat, and the sun tinged her cheeks with gold, like summer fruit. She was beautiful, and so young! Suddenly, a glare of panic came into Abassa's eyes. Her hands twitched restlessly. The cat jumped to the ground.

'When you are in Baghdad with Ja'far, do not tell him that I have lost his sons. He must not know this, and yet they are lost. I shall not find them again, I am certain, but for God's sake, do not say anything to him. I should be afraid of his anger.'

She was trembling. Her grandfather put his hand on her hair.

'Ahmed will say nothing, my child, and we shall find your sons again. Be at peace!'

She seemed suddenly to grow calm and again turned

her head to the window. She no longer saw me, she did not even know that I was beside her.

'Come!' said my host.

And we went out.

I had lost everything when my master died, but Abassa had lost even more. The tears fell down my cheeks. So, there was nothing left of the past. Everything had been sacked, impounded, destroyed. Harun had won, but I knew that the taste of this victory was so bitter that it sickened him. Had he seen this little sister that he claimed to love so well? What then did he feel when he thought of her?

I left. Of Abassa, I kept only the eternal memory of a certain expression and of a mass of curly hair lit up by the sunlight that filtered through a sculpted wooden mashrabiyah. I declined the offer to stay at the old man's house. What would I have done there? No one needed me any more.

The Baghdad night shrouded Ahmed in its silence. Only the distant song of a woman could be heard, a guttural and joyous sound. There was a laugh, a man called out a name and the voice fell silent. Never before had the sky shone with so many fires. The moon, which was rising, lit up the façades of the houses round the square like a white and brown braid, picked out here and there in the purple of the braziers whose glowing red embers made spots of light on the dark ground, flowers strangely alive in the deserted and naked garden of the sleeping town. Suddenly, in the distance, there was a noise – a precise noise, strange at this time of night. Two horses were galloping, and the noise was swelling, loud against the prevailing silence: it filled the whole square, making people scatter and turn their heads.

Then, two men appeared, veiled, dressed in black. Were they one-eyed? Some of the people would later confirm this fact, but no one really saw them. The wind from their gallop swelled their galabiyas, and it was as if they were floating on the night like apparitions, or like mirages in the full desert sun. Ahmed saw them and did not move. He simply pulled his kuffiya over his face, hiding it from human eyes, and waited. The horsemen rode through the scattering crowd. The women and children fled. All this happened in silence. It was as if every gesture, every movement became slow, absorbed by time, water drunk up by the sand as soon as it had fallen, note of music dying on the still string of a cithara.

In front of the old storyteller, the horsemen came to a halt. One of them raised his sabre, a beautiful steel sabre with a pommel of turquoise.

'The caliph's ears are irritated by your folly, and he desires that you be silent for evermore. It is time for you to go back to those dogs you once served and whose name must never again be pronounced by anyone.'

The sabre swished down. The old beggar was so frail, so light, that the blade cut into his shoulder at the collar-bone. He remained upright in his sitting position but, already, his eyes had lost their sight. Then, striking a second time, the horseman cut off his head and it rolled on to the little prayer mat. The gaping eyes were looking to the west, there, beyond the river, to a deserted palace that a man had loved in times past.

The crowd dispersed and the hoof beats died out into the night. The square was deserted, the silence total. That night, in Baghdad, an old man had died, a poor and humble man in the round town with three walls, Baghdad like an old woman drowsing in forgotten times, and who, for the space of ten nights, had been roused from her dreams by an old storyteller. Dawn was not far off. A cock crowed and a dog walked up to the slumping body and began to lick the blood.

From the top of a minaret, the voice of a muezzin intoned the first call to prayer and was followed from mosque to mosque by other voices, as by an echo, and the ramparts became tinged with purple, as they had every morning at the gates of Khurasan and Basra, since Al-Mansur first set his eyes on that land.